SWEET SUNSETS

A SWEETGUM MEADOWS ROMANCE BOOK 2

IMANI PRICE

First Edition: March 2023

ISBN 978-1-957989-92-1 (ebook)
ISBN 978-1-957989-93-8 (paperback)

Published by Books to Hook Publishing, LLC.
www.BooksToHook.com

CONTENTS

CHAPTER ONE

Brandi walked down the sidewalk from the library, having just returned some of her books. She was on her way to Rochelle's Old-Fashioned Diner for her book club meeting, eager to talk to the other members about their latest romance read, an African-American Western titled *The Midnight Farm*.

The town of Sweetgum Meadows was quiet that Monday night; the biting frigid February air nipped at her nose as she gripped her book to her chest as if that could hold in some of her body heat. A blast of wind sent strands of her flat-ironed hair flying as she reached up to tuck them back into her low bun. She approached Main Street, waving kindly at a passerby walking his dog. It was the familiar face of Mr. Lewis wearing khaki trousers, a sweater with his white shirt collar peeking out, and a newsboy hat; his trusty Jack-Russel terrier Cornelius walked beside him. Brandi saw them every Monday evening on this walk. They exchanged a quick and friendly greeting before moving on.

When the weather was nice, she'd stop and chat with him, but they were both in a hurry to get to their destinations on this frigid evening. As Brandi crested the slight incline up to the Main Street sidewalk, the wind became stronger and colder. A few cars drove by slowly as she waited for the traffic light to change. She stood on the sidewalk, Sweetgum Daycare and Pre-K Center, where she worked to her right, and Demetrius' increasingly popular shop, Nerd Central Comics and Video Game Store, to her left. Finally, the traffic light turned red, so she hiked up her comfortably long and cozy skirt and trekked across the wet and empty street.

Once across, Brandi paused under the warm glow of Rochelle's Old-Fashioned Diner's red and blue neon sign to appreciate its ambiance. She admired how the lights created an ethereal glow on the brown skin of her hands. The building was an old, authentic diner built in the 1930s in New Jersey by Rochelle's great-grandparents. According to Rochelle, they had it transported to Sweetgum when her family moved to the area about seventy years ago. Rochelle loved to talk about her memories of her great-grandparents as a small child. Brandi liked to hear Rochelle's tales, being a sucker for romance and stories.

As the door chimed, signaling her arrival, the string of chatter from the diners greeted her along with a welcome burst of warm, delicious-smelling air from the cooking food. "There's your last member," Rochelle called cheerfully from behind the white and red counter lined with barstools. Brandi loved the diner's décor and its black and white checkerboard floor.

Brandi walked over to Rochelle as she made her way from behind the counter. Rochelle smiled happily, her bright white smile contrasting her dark brown skin. She was approaching the age of sixty, but you wouldn't know it by looking at her. She had her shoulder-length salt-and-pepper hair styled in two-strand twists and could have passed for forty. "How are you, dear? Were you at the library just now?"

"Yes, I had to return a few books," Brandi told her as she embraced Rochelle gently.

"The girls are at the booth in the back waiting," Rochelle smiled, pointing back over Brandi's shoulder.

"Thank you, Rochelle," Brandi said as Rochelle got back to work. As part of Brandi's upbringing, she was raised to put Ms., Mrs., and Mr. in front of the name of her elders, but Rochelle made it clear that she wanted to skip that formality and just to call her by her name.

Brandi turned to see the members of the book club: her three best friends, Joanne, Nevaeh, and Courtney; Mrs. Mei Zhang, an older Chinese-American woman who ran Sweet and Spicy Chinese Palace, the local Chinese restaurant; Kim, a local hairdresser and good friend; and a few of the "hit-and-run" squad of fit, older women who frequently power-walked the streets of Sweetgum—Mrs. Oliva Andrews, Mrs. Cecilia Bridges, and Mrs. Ethel Craskin. They were pleasant and loved to gossip, but if you were in their way when they walked the sidewalks, school track, or anywhere else they were power-walking, you'd better move out of the way. Random out-of-towners found that out the hard way, and it always entertained the locals as they were bull-dozed by the "hit-and-run" squad. Brandi knew them well, as they often came to the library to chat and pick up one of their other squad members, Mrs. Everly Williams, the local librarian.

Brandi, Joanne, Nevaeh, Courtney, and Kim were all in their early to mid-twenties. The other women in the book club were around their late fifties to early sixties. They were a motley crew, but they wouldn't have it any other way.

"It's about time," Joanne smirked, waving Brandi over, her beautiful riotous curls framing her face. "We ordered you a hot cocoa but waited to get food." Joanne was the owner of Roasted Beans Coffee Spot, the local coffee shop.

"Sorry about that." Brandi smiled, sliding into the largest

booth in the place. It was U-shaped, easily sat ten grown men, and took up half of the extension that Rochelle's father had added over thirty years ago. It was a classic diner piece and rare to find, so Rochelle took extra-good care of it and only used it for local meetings and special occasions.

"So, now that we're all here," Mrs. Zhang said, raising her hand to get the attention of everyone at the table, her long black hair with auburn highlights pulled back into a low ponytail. The highlights were Kim's idea at the last book club meeting. She was wearing a cable-knit sweater dress with leggings and had her reading glasses on the edge of her nose as she looked at the book in her hand. "We can begin discussing our read for the first half of this month—*The Midnight Farm*. First, let's talk about the characters before we decide to order some food."

"I liked the protagonist, though she seemed a bit lost, clumsy even," Courtney commented, starting them off. Her long, loose curls bounced slightly as she spoke, her outfit of jeans and a paint-stained t-shirt a bit light for the recent weather. "I mean, she was just destined to be put into a dangerous situation, and look what happened… dangerous situation."

"I agree; her character development was way too predictable." Nevaeh nodded, her sleek, silk-pressed hair cascading past her shoulders. She had on warm but brightly colored sweatpants and a hoodie. "I mean, she's set up to be saved by the hero right from the beginning, and I think it would have worked better for the character if she'd have been a bit more…."

"She needed a backbone, plain and simple," Kim said, her box braids beautifully arranged into a top bun. She always had the best hair in town, and Brandi always admired her for that. She also admired that Kim had recently had her own romantic encounter with the man of her dreams.

"I agree, she was a bit too fragile," Mrs. Andrews said, nodding and swiping the bang of her gray pixie bob from her eyes. She wore a pink and navy tracksuit, as did the other two members of the "hit-and-run" squad. They tended to match their clothing as if they were a power-walking gang.

"But that's who she is," Joanne replied passionately, shaking her head. "Felicia is a fragile, somewhat soft-spoken, but kind-hearted woman who enjoys and lives a simple life. That's who she is—you can't change that just because you would have approached the situation differently. The question isn't whether the character development was predictable—the question is whether or not the character developed at all."

"Of course she did," Mrs. Zhang chuckled, shaking her head. "A character develops in every story. That's the point of most stories, especially romances."

"And that development was predictable and a bit boring," Kim said. Mrs. Bridges and Craskin nodded their agreement.

"That hero wasn't, though," Courtney smirked, making Joanne chuckle. "I mean, can we just talk about Simon?" she said, fanning herself dramatically.

"It seems everyone is interested in our hero, Simon," Nevaeh laughed. "He was quite the man. The chapter where he saves her from that horse in the corral?"

"Oh, I know," Joanne sighed, picking up her glass of sweet tea. "I thought for sure she was going to tear his clothes off right there."

"She should have," Mrs. Craskin laughed, making them all chuckle and clap their approval. She had a sassy look on her face with her short hair styled in fingerwaves. They were a somewhat rowdy bunch, but the rest of the local diners didn't seem to mind them.

"If I were fifteen years younger," Mrs. Bridges smirked, tucking a long silver loc behind her ear.

"He *was* chiseled from stone, like a warrior," Kim admitted, flipping through the book. "But his line about her heart belonging to him, and how he wanted her to rip his own heart from his chest, so he didn't have to long for her anymore…."

"That! Yes, that beautiful line…oh, and you know he wasn't innocent," Joanne smirked, glancing over at Brandi, who had remained quiet this whole time.

"His character was domineering, a boss, and somewhat dangerous," Courtney smiled, looking down at the book's cover. "I mean, think about it. He's a hard-working rancher who knows three things—cattle, horses, and women. But of course, he was nothing but trouble, making him so irresistible to the reader."

"But was he that irresistible?" Brandi asked softly. Only Joanne, who was sitting next to her, heard.

"What'd you say, Brandi?" she asked, encouraging everyone else to stop chatting and listen.

"I mean, was he that irresistible? Objectively?" Brandi asked, looking down at the book cover. "Yes, he's a rough, tough, and emotionally stunted man with the body of a warrior, but my question is—was that intentional? Did the writer make Felicia so vanilla and bland that Simon glowed and practically pulsed by comparison? And why would the writer do that, if not to expose the fact that perhaps this relationship would not work out as the reader thought?"

"What do you mean?" Kim asked, genuinely curious, her honey-brown eyes watching Brandi.

"I mean, the ending was inconclusive," Brandi replied, feeling a bit more confident. "Sure, they hooked up. He finally said those three words Felicia wanted to hear, but that doesn't really mean anything without some sort of conclusion. The writer just left it open-ended after he went to find her at the bus station. They kiss, and then what? Nothing…"

"Is there a sequel?" Courtney asked, sounding a bit shocked. "I didn't even realize any of that…."

"No, no, no. The writer clearly meant it to be a happily ever after," Mrs. Zhang said, the other three older women agreeing. "They found one another, faced some challenges, decided to have faith and trust in their love for one another, and that's the happily ever after. Of course, they'll get married and do everything else people do because that's what people do. That's the purpose of the writer's ending and their meaning—you can find love in everyday life."

"That's beautiful, Mrs. Zhang," Kim admitted, Brandi agreeing. "I hadn't even thought of it like that."

"Wow, good point," Nevaeh said, mischief alight in her face. "But now I think we need to discuss something that all of us are thinking."

"What's that?" Courtney asked, eyebrow raised in suspicion.

"What do we all look for in a man?" Nevaeh asked as if casually inquiring about the next community fundraiser.

"I have my man," Mrs. Zhang said proudly. "He's practical, romantic, and every year since we got married, he gives me roses and irises on our anniversary, my birthday, mother's day, and the days our children were born."

"I want that," Neveah sighed, leaning against the table on her elbow. "That's so sweet...."

"My husband is a quiet man, hard-working, and doesn't express his feelings in words," Mrs. Andrews smiled, gaining all their attention. "But that spark of creativity and adventure that had drawn me to him almost forty years ago resurfaces, and I fall in love all over again."

"My husband is quite traditional," Mrs. Bridges smiled, a nostalgic twinkle in her eye. "But he isn't home a lot, driving the truck up and down the coast. Of course, the family and I miss him, but he's the light of our lives when he is home. He's loving, outspoken, and loves to spend time with all of us. He's the rock our family is built upon...."

"Jack is an angry old goat," Mrs. Craskin smirked, waving for Rochelle to come over and take their orders. "He's often cranky and doesn't care for people too much, but I'll say this for the stubborn old ox… he's one hell of a lover."

"Oh, lord, TMI!" Brandi blushed, everyone bursting out into laughter. The members were still chuckling, lively and energetic after their meal and another hour of chatter. The group disbanded after they revealed the book for the next meeting in two weeks, an adventurous romance featuring an international con artist and a savvy writer who was a former executive traveling to find herself.

After a little more discussion, the "hit and run" crew left. It was just past seven, and Brandi, Neveah, Courtney, Joanne, Mrs. Zhang, and Kim all sat at the table, debating whether to order cake or pie to split between them. After choosing a piece of peach, apple, and pumpkin pie, the six munched happily, discussing further the requirements of a good man.

"It's a bit ironic, though," Nevaeh said, taking a bite of pumpkin pie. "Here we all are, single, discussing the requirements of our ideal romance."

"I most definitely am *not* single," Kim reminded them, making Brandi smile.

"I would be happy to set you ladies up with any of my sons or nephews, or perhaps Rochelle and I can help you find a man," Mrs. Zhang said, sipping her decaf coffee.

"No, definitely not," Joanne smirked, making Mrs. Zhang wink. Joanne lowered her voice now, speaking for everyone at the table. "We know Rochelle means well, but she is a very poor matchmaker."

"She's slightly clumsy," Mrs. Zhang agreed, setting her cup down. "But I'm here to help! And we could find you the most eligible men in town, including my second-eldest son, who's attending the University of Georgia as a sophomore this year. Architect, smart boy, not so lucky with ladies, I think."

"She's just trying to help," Kim assured, smiling as Rochelle approached.

"And I'll remind you that my partner here might be very straightforward with her attempts to match-make," Rochelle said, picking up on the conversation as she handed out the dinner checks. "But it was me who sent Kim on that awful date to the State Park, which led her to her current stud and the love of her life, Malik."

"I guess that's true," Kim laughed, smiling happily up at Rochelle. Her bright eyes twinkled. "If you hadn't set me up with such a jerk, he wouldn't have abandoned me in the middle of nowhere. If that hadn't happened, I wouldn't have met my sexy park ranger."

"See, I rest my case," Rochelle said, throwing up her hands in victory, then gathering up the various cash and cards on the table with the checks. "I'm clumsy, but I'll find you a match.

"That should be your motto." Joanne grinned, leaving her a five-dollar tip on the table.

"Your love story is like a fairy tale," Courtney sighed, looking over at Kim, her eyes dreamy. "Like one of the books that we read."

"How are things with you and Malik?" Nevaeh asked, paying close attention to Kim. "Is he coming out of his shell?"

"We're spending a lot of time together and learning about one another's interests," Kim admitted. "We're thinking of taking a trip together one of these days."

"Oh! A trip, where to?" Mrs. Zhang asked, stirring her newly filled decaf with cream.

"We want to see some of the country's national parks, so we'll head north to his old home before heading west." Her voice trilled with excitement. "It hasn't been set, but he also has some family and some skeletons to bring out of the closet where they are concerned."

"Oh, some family issues?"

"When his grandfather passed in his sleep, a distant relative inherited the cabin that Malik and his grandfather were living in because of some legal technicalities. Unfortunately, that relative wasn't very kind," Kim explained, sipping from her cup. "Malik wants to see if they can let bygones be bygones and get to know each other as a family since his grandfather was the only one he really knew. But the rest of the trip will be gorgeous."

"That trip would be perfect for your social media and Malik's YouTube channel," Joanne said, encouraging her to expand their business. Joanne was a businesswoman at heart, taking risks and opportunities when presented. She was also very good at changing the subject.

Brandi smiled at this, listening to them discuss the various state parks, ideal travel destinations, and the romance you could experience across the country. Mrs. Zhang was particularly interested in seeing the west coast and visiting her sister, who had moved there in the 80s. Brandi nodded along as the group laughed, chatted, and discussed their passions, but her mind was racing with romantic, somewhat fanciful thoughts.

Kim was so lucky to find someone who understood her, brought out the best she could offer, and encouraged her to be herself. Malik was a kind guy who Brandi had only met a few times. He was also nice to look at, which was something that didn't matter as much to Brandi. She'd be grateful for anyone to ask her out because she hadn't had a serious boyfriend since she was a senior in high school. She and her ex had gone to the same small college together but quickly grew apart. Since then, she'd met no one with whom she could be truly comfortable.

It was an odd feeling, feeling alone in a world full of pairs and families. Brandi was only twenty-three, so it wasn't like she was running out of time, but her patience had grown thin. She hadn't dated in college and focused solely on her career, loving her job as head teacher at Sweetgum Daycare and Pre-K Center. But, however much she loved her students, it still didn't stop her from feeling lonely. She had always wondered if that's why she liked romance novels so much, especially sweet romances, and if her happily ever after would come soon.

Her best friends Joanne, Nevaeh, and Courtney were all single as well, but they'd still go out on dates and have a good time. She'd go along occasionally, but mainly she was focused on her work and reading about the romantic endings in novels. A part of her was sick of only experiencing true romance through the pages of her books, and the other part knew that it was highly unlikely that she'd be swept off her feet in the real world. However, that didn't stop her from yearning for comforting arms, soft whispers, and some meaningful eye contact.

If the eyes were the gateway to the soul, then the imagination was the gateway to love, and Brandi had imagination and passion to spare. She just needed the man to come to sweep her off her feet, even if she felt that was a bit old-fashioned. Though, in Brandi's mind, that was exactly what she was—an old-fashioned southern romantic.

CHAPTER TWO

"Good morning, Tristan," Brandi greeted the toddling child as he walked in, holding the hand of his clearly pregnant mother.

"Miss Brandi!" he smiled, going to his small cubby with his extra-small backpack. His dark hair bounced atop his head as he passed by, his mother, Gabrielle, happily waving goodbye to him as he joined one of the three aids in the room beyond.

"How is it going?" Brandi asked, smiling at Gabrielle's full belly.

"Oh, it's pregnancy." She smiled wanly, patting her belly softly. "I'll be back early today and have your money order."

"Thanks, Gabrielle." Brandi smiled. "Little Tristan has been so helpful with the other students; he just melts my heart."

"He's always talking about Miss Brandi when his older sister talks about her day at school," Gabrielle laughed, turning from the room with a wave. "I'll see you in a few hours!"

"Have a good shift," Brandi called after her, another parent entering to drop their child off. They still had another six drop-offs, and Brandi was always at the front desk and reception area to welcome every parent and student.

She loved her job, greeting the toddlers and children every morning, getting them settled with breakfast in the main classroom, and directing their curiosity and skills. She had always found it a shame that more teachers and daycares didn't even address a child's imagination or curiosity, often settling them with structured lessons and group activities. They hardly paid attention to the individual, and that was Brandi's main focus in school, early childhood development being a fascination for her.

She had become the director and head teacher of the daycare two years ago when the older owner, Mrs. Bea, retired after thirty years. She was a remarkable but strict woman, a bit different in her approach to children. However, Mrs. Bea hired Brandi straight out of school as an assistant and groomed her to take Mrs. Bea's place. Mrs. Bea had helped raise the past three generations of children in Sweetgum, and none would forget her, especially since she still came in weekly with her seniors' group of five to six people from the local retirement home to read and play games with the toddlers.

"Welcome, Alysanna," Brandi welcomed a cute little curly-haired girl with big brown eyes.

"Morning, Miss Brandi." She smiled, skipping by to greet one of her friends.

"Have a good day, baby." Her mother smiled, waving and nodding at Brandi.

"Good morning, Jayden." Brandi smiled before turning to greet his father, a familiar Real Estate Agent named Joe.

"Mornin' Miss Brandi," the boy giggled, waving at his friend Tristan.

"I'll have next month's money order for you at pickup." Joe waved, smiling at his already engaged son. "He's always talking about class, and I can't tell you how much it means to us that you were able to coax him out of his shell."

"Well, a lot of children are dealing with anxiety and the feeling of isolation. It's a simple matter of understanding the cause and applying the right pressure to engage his interest," she said. "I'm always happy to have a successful and happy student."

"He loves your classes; I'm almost afraid to send him to the school next year," Joe said, waving as he left. "Thanks again, Brandi!"

"Morning, Miss Brandi!" a couple more students called, whizzing past her as parents dropped off and waved. One parent was on her phone deep in conversation, and the other was a busy dad who had just finished his overnight shift at the dispatch.

"Have a good sleep!" Brandi called after him as he grunted and threw a quick wave.

"I intend to! I've got all day. The wife is doing pick up," he said, walking back out with a low chuckle.

"Miss Brandi!" a familiar voice called, the little girl rushing up to her from the front door. She had a pair of glasses and held her favorite picture book. "Look! I've got a book for my bookshelf!"

"Congratulations, Maryana," Brandi gushed, hugging her back as the little girl hugged her leg.

"Go on, get your breakfast," her mother said, pointing at her cubby. "I'll see you later, baby."

"Bye, mom!" Maryana called after her, the woman waving politely at Brandi before leaving.

After the children were settled at their tables, the assistants floated between the groups that munched on their breakfast burritos and fruit cups. Brandi did the same, telling the students what they had planned for the day, including a combined naptime and storytime after lunch. The children were full of chatter, so the three assistants decided to divide them up between their three ages and get them started on a group activity.

Brandi walked between the three, each group picking a different activity, though all three groups usually gravitated to the board games. As the three groups set up their respective games, Brandi decided to get ahead on some paperwork. She had a new intake today, and the mother, Chelsea, very curtly told her that she'd drop off her son Grayson after nine, though drop off is traditionally anywhere between seven and eight. After Brandi faxed the paperwork to the state for their new intake and updated their records, she stapled together a welcome booklet, a magnet designed by Courtney, and the next yearly schedule, including planned outings, visitors, and meal chart.

Brandi was an organized person, and she'd found this was especially helpful when dealing with parents and their children as she was putting the finishing touch on the packet when the new mom and her son walked in. Since it was after nine, the children in the other room had already finished their breakfast and board games. Now, they were getting ready for outdoor time, which allowed Brandi to show off the facility.

"Good morning." Brandi smiled, offering her hand to Chelsea as they stood in the front room where the cubbies stood. "Everyone's headed outside for now, having finished their breakfast and group activity. Would you like to take your son outside first to meet the assistants?"

"No," the woman said flatly, checking her phone. She was dressed in tight, torn jeggings and a cropped and loose t-shirt. Her hair was expertly styled into long waterwaves draping down her back, and she wore heavy perfume and makeup.

Brandi turned her attention to the little boy. Chelsea's paperwork said her son was three, his big brown eyes darting about the room nervously as he stood beside his mother. Chelsea didn't spare him a glance as she looked around the front room critically while checking a dinging message on her phone.

"You've got all your state certifications, yes?" Chelsea asked, ignoring Brandi's hand until she lowered it.

"Yes, we're certified to operate within the county and state and are under capacity, hoping to expand next year with another assistant," Brandi explained, smiling kindly at the shy little boy.

"You've got cleaning services, yes? Nightly?"

"Yes, a local cleaning service comes in every night after we close to clean and sanitize," Brandi said, unsure why Chelsea was being so rude and curt.

"And your emergency protocols? Are you and your assistants trained in active-shooter drills and CPR?"

"Y-yes." Brandi stuttered, a bit taken aback by her tone. "We've got an automatic alarm system that calls into our security company, and they notify local dispatch. We've got a comprehensive set of drills we practice, and I think many of your questions can be answered by this booklet and welcome packet."

Brandi handed the bag containing the packet to her with a smile, but she just looked inconvenienced, opening the small bag and looking at the pamphlet. Her son still looked very nervous, his eyes firmly glued on the room beyond where all the toys and games were. Then, after a few moments of glancing through the materials, she looked at the meal schedule, her nose wrinkling immediately.

"Grayson, go play outside; mommy will see you later," she dismissed, nudging him with her leg as she squinted at the meal menus.

The little boy hesitated, a sad haze in his eyes as he slowly shuffled off into the other room alone. Brandi didn't need time to think, reacting instinctively.

"I'll be right back," she insisted, leaving the annoyed and bewildered Chelsea in the front room as she escorted Grayson to the other children outside. She gently explained to him what their small, varied play yard included. She even handed him a snack early: a gluten-free packet of veggie chips.

He smiled, but she noticed he didn't seem sure what to do next, standing on the sidelines as one of the assistants, Shea, encouraged him to engage with the other excited children in his age group. He was slow at it but eventually offered to share his chips with Maryana. That's when Brandi went back inside, seeing Chelsea in the main playroom, investigating everything closely.

"Are these used toys?" Chelsea asked, pointing at some of the older toys from the seventies and eighties that Mrs. Bea kept.

"Some of them are from the previous director," Brandi said, showing her the picture of Mrs. Bea and several groups of her students, all on the large wall that featured a single picture of each class she'd taught from 1989 – 2019.

"You should get some newer toys for the children, especially after the madness that was 2020." She shrugged, inspecting the blackboard and whiteboard. Then, before moving to the kitchens, she inspected a few of the game shelves and the tall bookshelf.

"You serve gluten-free?"

"Yes, we have gluten-free, sugar-free, caffeine-free, and vegetarian options," Brandi said, watching her inspect the refrigerators and the oven.

"You should hire a nutritionist," she said, her nose wrinkled at the old but clean kitchen. "You definitely need an upgrade in here."

Brandi was once again taken aback, remaining pleasant as Chelsea crossed the playroom again and inspected the naptime chamber, an ocean-themed room of individual roll-out memory foam mats aligned all around in a semi-circle. There was a comfortable rocking chair set at the other end, and the lights and noises in the room were full of trickling water and hazy blues and greens. Chelsea walked over to the dark blue blind and opened it, peeping out before walking back across the room back into the main room.

Brandi was giving Chelsea the benefit of the doubt; perhaps she was nervous about leaving her child in a strange new place. However, it was possible that she was just being abrasive and entitled, so Brandi needed to figure out how to confront it without causing problems. Chelsea's suggestions quickly became demands as she inspected the three bathrooms along the main room's front wall.

"Yeah, this bathroom needs to be redone. That tile is all wrong," she groaned, turning away. "I thought you said you remodeled?"

"Four years ago, before Mrs. Bea retired," Brandi explained, pointing at the addition of storage and the landscaping in the yard. "She put money into the basement, turning it into a storm shelter and movie theater. It's in the history portion of the welcome booklet...."

"Right," Chelsea replied, her voice dismissive. "Just make sure Grayson doesn't share food with his classmates. It's disgusting, and I don't want some other kid's germs coming home with us. We've had enough of that kind of thing...."

"Sicknesses tend to burn through the whole class if they are exposed," Brandi said, noticing that the groups were coming back inside. "We insist parents keep their child home if they have symptoms."

"I hope that day comes out of the fees," Chelsea snapped, turning back toward the front room. "He has to have sunblock on when he goes outside, no matter for how long. He's got some in his bag."

"That's not a problem. We make safety a priority," Brandi said, following her back out to the entrance. "I'm glad you're asking questions and becoming involved. It's encouraging to see parents be so involved."

"What else would I be?" she snapped, rolling her eyes at her.

"Well, I should get to my day. The children are ready to start their lessons," Brandi said, turning to move back behind the small reception desk.

"Yeah, yeah," Chelsea replied, waving her hand dismissively as she stared at her phone. "What kind of discounts do you offer for public servants? His grandpa is an EMT…."

"Well, the discount would only apply if it's the legal guardian or parent," Brandi explained, becoming impatient.

"What about a low-income?" she asked, texting and scrolling through her phone.

"There is an application for state aid to pay for costs; I'll just need you to go to our website and, under forms and documents, follow the link to the state's daycare assistance program," Brandi said, watching her stuff the welcome packet roughly into her bag. "But I should probably get back to the students."

"Do you have an on-site nurse or someone who can administer medications?" she questioned, glancing up at Brandi. "Grayson is allergic to bees."

"My assistant, Shea, is CPR and medically certified to administer medications and address any medical emergencies," Brandi assured, gaining Shea's attention as she helped settle the children in for their first lesson for the day. "We're about to start our first lesson, so I should probably get in there. I hope you read over the—. "

"You've got a fax? And internet? I'm getting Grayson a cellphone, so I need him to be able to access his network or the internet to stay in contact," she explained, looking over the front office and meeting eyes with Brandi. "Well? Wifi? Yes?"

"Yes, the employees usually use it, and we stream movies once a week for the children," Brandi replied, becoming irritated. She had never considered herself a pushover, although she never liked confrontation, but the way Chelsea was inspecting everything, and interrupting her, was infuriating. She needed to get her out of there so she could start her day with the children, but Chelsea just wouldn't take the hint.

Brandi wondered how she was going to get her out of there without making a scene in front of the waiting class of children.

But then, Chelsea's phone rang, and she picked it up, her flat tone immediately changing to a bubbly, excited one. She seemed almost a different person, answering whoever it was with enthusiasm.

"Hey, I'm dropping Grayson off, then I'll be there," she explained, glancing at Brandi. "Just inspecting and making sure the place is legit. There weren't many reviews online, and it seems a bit old."

Shea was standing in the doorway now, watching bewildered as Chelsea turned to the door and left, not even bothering to say goodbye or when she would be back; Brandi could not even tell her she needed to sign the pages included in her welcome packet. Brandi was still bewildered as Shea approached, her nose wrinkled in disgust.

"She's going to be a problem," Shea whispered, turning back to the room of waiting children with a smile. "You'll need to nip that in the bud and quick."

"How?" Brandi asked, feeling tired already, plastering a happy smile on her face for the waiting young faces.

It was shortly after four, and Brandi and her assistants were cleaning up the toys, mess, and chaos at the end of the day. Brandi let Shea handle checkouts and was content to clean up and say goodbye to the lingering students finishing their art projects. She, Lehna, and Alyza were all cleaning when Shea returned to the main room, looking a bit concerned.

"What's up?" Brandi asked, hoping none of the children or parents had problems getting home.

"Grayson's still here," Shea explained, nodding at the shy,

sad-looking little boy sitting near his cubby, waiting for his mom. "Chelsea isn't answering any of my calls or texts."

"You need to stand up to her when she gets here," Lehna said, shaking her head. Lehna and Alyza had heard about what happened from Shea. "She's taking advantage and hurting her child in the process."

"I can't tell someone how to parent their own child," Brandi scoffed. "You saw her earlier."

"You're too nice," Alyza scoffed back. "I'll do it if you won't."

"That'd be inappropriate," Brandi sighed, glancing at the child. "And I don't want him to think this is a hostile place."

"He seems withdrawn, and I feel bad for him," Alyza said, her eyes becoming a bit misty. "He's a polite little darling, and his mom treats him like that."

"It's my responsibility to confront her," Brandi insisted, squaring her shoulders and putting away the last of the colorful building blocks. "I'll go wait with him. You guys finish up and go home."

"You sure?" Shea asked; she and the other two a bit skeptical.

"I hope she's here in time for me to get to the library," Brandi said, glancing at her bag and jacket in the small office space behind the desk. "I've got some interlibrary loans, and if she doesn't get here soon, I won't get there before they close."

"Calm down; you'll get your romance novel fix," Lehna said, the four of them giggling. "I could set you up with my cousin, you know? He's just graduated with a master's degree in engineering. Wants to live in Florida, design bridges and seawalls or something."

"That's tempting," Brandi admitted, admiring his drive to help others. In truth, she really wanted to meet someone and fall in love, and the thought of an engineer with a big heart sounded almost too good to be true. She wondered why he was still single.

"Nonsense, my brother's a better option, and he just got back from a year in Australia," Shea smirked.

"I can't," Brandi said, shaking her head. "I'll find my own dates, but I appreciate the thought. Dating a co-worker's family is a recipe for disaster. For now, I'm going to see if Grayson is okay."

The three of them waved at her as they prepared to leave, and she went to sit next to Grayson in one of the cubbies with a smile. He glanced up at her with his big brown eyes before staring back at the small backpack in his lap.

"You okay?"

"Mom's always late," he whispered, his voice barely audible. "I'll get kicked out of here, too."

"You were in another place before this, right?" Brandi asked, still cheerful and kind. "Did you like it?"

"I did, but mommy was late every day," he said, glancing up at her again. "Sorry."

Brandi was surprised by his ability to express himself at such a young age and also found his word usage advanced for someone of only three. It was curious as he was slightly taller than those in his group. Perhaps his birthday was recorded wrong, or he was just advanced for his age. Either way, Brandi was happy to sit and talk with him until his mom arrived.

After ten more minutes, a discussion about his favorite activities and his older cousin, whom he spent a lot of time with, Chelsea finally showed up. It was almost four-thirty, and Brandi rarely stayed this late, usually spending her evenings at the library until they closed at six. Chelsea came bouncing through the door, makeup slightly smudged and hair wild as she spoke loudly with whoever was on her phone.

"Yeah, I just got to the daycare, picking up Grayson." She smiled, waving at the boy as he ran to her side with his back-pack. She had her large purse over her arm and stuffed his bag inside it, waving at Brandi as she stood dumbfounded by Chelsea's behavior.

"Chelsea, I need to speak with you for a moment," Brandi said, stepping forward, but Chelsea didn't stop, continuing to speak into her phone as she waved back at her again.

"Sorry, no time," she finally uttered, opening the daycare door and motioning for Grayson to follow.

"It's important," Brandi called after her, but it was useless; Chelsea grabbed her son's hand and disappeared from the doorway.

"Wow," Shea said, making Brandi jump. All three of them were still there, watching the door in disbelief.

Now Brandi was angry, confused, and embarrassed, an odd combination she couldn't quite understand. She was being walked all over in front of her assistant teachers, and she didn't even know how to break through to this woman. She felt horrible for Grayson but felt even worse for herself.

She was frustrated as she left, engaging the security system before walking with the other girls around the corner of the building to the parking lot. After saying goodbye to the others, Brandi considered what to do. She was stressed and annoyed and didn't know how to approach a woman like Chelsea. She had a strong and domineering personality toward everyone, including her own child.

After several moments sitting in her small sedan, she pulled out, driving down the block toward the library. She needed to pick up her books and relax. She was more than excited to dig into some new books by some of her favorite romance authors. Pulling into the small parking lot, she grabbed her bag, shutting off the car, and felt that familiar sense of home. The library was her favorite place on earth. Hoisting her cloth bag and purse over her jacketed shoulder, she strode up to the familiar red brick building, eager to open the new pages.

CHAPTER THREE

"Ｗhat in the world...." Chris was standing behind the library desk; his grandmother's old computer system was so obsolete it was almost insane. She had upgraded to computers over fifteen years ago, but her system seemed to haven't been updated since, and the inter-library loan system was convoluted and slow.

He had only been in Sweetgum a week and struggled desperately to find himself in his hometown. He had been roped into helping his granny at the library, a job he didn't mind having. He'd spent the past six years in California, attending UCLA for his Ph.D., focusing on library sciences and the African-American contribution to the field. He was also very interested in little-known parts of history and how they fit into a culture's dominant social and political ideology.

However, it was only his first day filling in for his grandmother, who was feeling under the weather. She was the librarian in their small town, and her computer system absolutely stumped him. He'd been trying to figure it out all day, hoping to upgrade it so they could use it seamlessly. However, the more he played with settings and software updates, the more he doubted that was possible. He hoped it worked, glancing up at the clock to see it was just after four, less than two hours until the library closed.

The library was fairly quiet, with a wave of students arriving after school, followed by a few older folks for a read-along, and some regulars like Demetrius, the comic bookstore owner, who frequently obtained fantasy and science fiction works through interlibrary loan. Chris had known Demetrius since they were in school, even though Demetrius had been a few grades ahead of him; the older student was his guide to some of his favorite cultural icons and fandoms. Chris scratched his dark beard, smoothing the goatee as he considered what the computers were doing. His simple blue button-up shirt and yellow-gold tie felt too formal for his small hometown library.

As a child, he had come to the library a lot; his grandma always babysat him after school. She'd be here, among old books, older ladies, and their book club, often chatting and gossiping as he read quietly in her office or on one of the old couches. Chris was the only grandchild that really appreciated the library. His other siblings were readers but less enthusiastic about education than he was. He was the oldest of six siblings and usually felt most responsible for them, helping his granny watch them after school until his parents got off from work.

After college, his Ph.D. program, and traveling a bit of the west coast, Chris was back home, ready to enjoy his hometown again. He'd been on the grind, working day in and day out, for six years to complete his education ahead of schedule. He thought he'd go into academia, graduating in the top 25% of his graduating class at UCLA, but all he really wanted was to come home. He didn't know what he wanted to do with his advanced degree in tiny Sweetgum, but he knew that this was where he just wanted to be, where he wanted to live the rest of his life, hopefully with a big family one day.

His pride in his studies and his understanding of his place in this world only highlighted the fact that he was happy back home. Though beautiful, he wanted things that the wider world could not give him. His comfort back home, goals, and aspirations for a better career had all mingled, and he had wondered what he could make work in this tiny hometown. He could find a job as a museum curator in a nearby city or in Atlanta and had considered several jobs and positions in larger cities.

Sweetgum also had a strong connection to his passions, being an old town that former slaves founded after the Civil War. The town was started when two Black women, both widows, set out to live far away from civilization. They wanted to live peacefully on their own and raise their children on a small farm. With so much rural space in Georgia, they simply found a plot of land that wasn't part of any jurisdiction. But, there was far more to it, and it was here in this library, in the archives of the city hall and record rooms, that he found his passion for the subject of history. Particularly his own heritage and his family's role in the town. That just led him down a path of enchantment as he quickly branched out into regional and then national history. He even became intrigued, almost obsessed, with the underrepresented and little-known Victorian-era African-American writers.

Chris sighed as he noticed the computer was being slower than it had been before, the update finally initiating on the slow but steady connection. He was pretty sure this library needed new hardware. He had no idea how his grandmother got by like this and wondered if he'd have to revert to paper and stamp records in order to check out and receive books. That wouldn't go well in the state system where the books were registered digitally.

After rechecking the system to see that the update had stalled out, Chris huffed in frustration before scanning some books to organize them on a rolling cart. He needed to check them back into the state system and replace them on their various shelves. Walking down the aisles between the tall and old cedar shelves brought back that familiar feeling of home, causing a smile to spread over his face. The smell of pages, cedar, and this library's particular earthy floral potpourri was heady, making him grateful to be back. He had a chance to see a lot of his old friends already, remembering the past weekend.

When Chris returned, his friend Nate gathered all of their old friends, and his enthusiastic and loud personality caused a party to form at Nate's house. It was all right; his dad had the biggest house in town and was the mayor, so it became a block party for the entire town. Nate invited everyone he could find, with Chris' extroverted best friend making a big deal about his return home. Chris' mom made her famous beef ribs, his granny made five batches of macaroni and cheese, and the various neighbors and family members brought huge dishes of food and coolers of drinks.

It was a huge party, taking up much of the yard, but he was so happy to catch up with friends and family that he ignored the jibes Nate's father made about the damage to the lawn. What he enjoyed, aside from the giant Saturday night party, was the Sunday afternoon dinner at his granny's. There were leftovers everywhere, and he and his six siblings, their families, his parents, and granny all sat down to a feast after church. It was the first service Chris had attended since Christmas two years ago, and he missed it terribly.

He and his brothers sat around with his nephews watching football, the children running in and out of the house as the day wore on and the games heated up. Various people wanted him to come outside or into the kitchen. He'd oblige, leaving his brothers to their drinks and football as he mingled with every-one, including curious neighbors and his granny's pastor, the youthful Leon. He missed eating wings with them and spending quiet Sundays on various couches.

He was putting the last of the books away when he heard the

door to the library jingle and glanced at the clock to see it was almost five. He had been taking his time putting books away, the small and cozy library seeming cavernous when empty. He emerged from one of the aisles, pushing his cart, called out a kind greeting, and put away the last of the youth fantasy fiction before emerging.

Standing at the counter was a gorgeous woman he didn't recognize. Her radiant brown skin was flawless, her eyes widening slightly as she caught sight of him and realized she was dealing with a stranger. She had the most intense brown eyes he'd ever seen. She gave a small smile as she lowered her gaze bashfully.

"H-hello," she stuttered, biting her lip before her eyes darted around nervously. He was absolutely smitten.

"Hi, sorry to startle you; I'm Chris, Everly's grandson." He smiled, stretching out his hand. "She's feeling under the weather, so I said I'd take over the library for a few days."

"Oh, hi, Chris," she said, extending her hand as he pushed the cart back behind the desk. He leaned over it, taking her hand firmly and shaking it. "Nice to meet you. I'm Brandi, your granny's number one customer."

"My role has been usurped," he said, smiling at her.

"I've got some interlibrary loan holds to pick up," she said, pulling out her library card and placing it on the desk. "They should be on the reserve shelf, in the back. Probably came in yesterday with the weekly delivery."

"Number one customer, indeed." He smirked, turning to the small room behind the desk and finding the shelf. "So, you a fellow librarian or a local enthusiast?"

"Both, in a way," she said, watching him grab her books. "I love reading, always have. Been coming here since I was a child."

"Same," he said, turning to look at her again.

"Is she terribly sick?" Brandi asked, leaning against the high desk as he scanned her books carefully.

"She seems to be in top form but insists she's got a fever and sore throat," he shrugged, glancing up at her. "She's overly cautious, understandably."

"I can understand that," she said, hoisting her bag over her shoulder tighter.

Chris nodded and glanced down at the screen after scanning her library card. Handing it back to her, he offered to bag up her books, but she refused, opening the bag hanging over her shoulder for him. After maneuvering all four in, he turned back to the screen, ensuring everything was in order before closing the system. To his surprise, it said that Brandi owed some fines. At that moment, he was sorely tempted to wave them, allowing her to have her current books without issue. However, he needed to be professional, realizing he'd become entirely too enthralled by her charms. Furthermore, he needed to be fair to everyone who used the library and returned their books on time.

"Brandi, I'm sorry, but the system says you have late fees," he explains, pointing to the screen. "You can have your holds as soon as you pay for those."

"What?" she asked, her eyebrows rising in disbelief. "That's impossible; I've never had a late return in my life. So it must be a mistake."

"It says you owe almost $15," he insisted, pointing at the screen again. "It's right here."

"No, that's impossible," she reiterated, eyes narrowed as she glanced at the screen. "I come to the library several times a week, so there is no way I owe fines."

"I don't know what to tell you," he said, becoming slightly frustrated at her stubbornness. "Look, it says you owe for all of these."

"What? I was just here four days ago and took out new books. There is no way I owe. They are right there in the return bin!"

"Look, I'm only telling you what it says here on the screen," he said tightly, unwilling to back down. "You owe for *Rushing Waters Ranch*, *The Horseman's Hat*, *Nights In Savannah*, *Terra's Lover*...."

$\mathcal{B}$randi's face immediately flushed with embarrassment, the hot feeling there amplified by the sultry drawl of his Georgia accent as he read the titles. This handsome man wearing rectangular glasses that should have made him look nerdy, with his immaculate trimmed hair and his dark brown eyes, could see her reading history!

Of course, she'd noticed how handsome he was the second she walked in. Those dark eyes behind black frames accentuated the dark goatee and beard on his perfectly dark skin. He'd had a wide white smile and beautiful sparkling eyes. Brandi also noticed he was quite casually dressed, his tall, wiry frame casting a shadow as he rubbed his hand across his close-cropped hair. She had to concentrate on not fainting when he kept reading through her clearly romantic book selections.

"Wait, wait," Brandi finally spoke, shaking her head as she came around the desk. She gently moved him to the side, anxious to get to the computer. She needed to get herself out of this embarrassing situation! His grandmother never judged her on her book choices and always made her feel at ease. She couldn't believe this stunning man was casually reading off her romance novel reading history.

"See," she finally explained, pointing at the column of numbers. "This column is fines owed; this next one is the cost of the book itself, should it not be returned."

"Ooh," he said, eyes wide at the screen behind his glasses. He squinted briefly before flushing with embarrassment. "I'm sorry; I didn't mean to accuse you of anything. This is only my first day using the system."

"It's all right; I'm very familiar with the system," she said, trying to put him at ease. "I've spent weeks volunteering at the library over the years."

"Then why does it show me that?" he groaned, shaking his head. "This system is a bit outdated, but I know granny would never be able to figure out the new system."

"The new system is confusing," she agreed, pointing at the screen. "I updated her before, but she was so confused I had to uninstall it again."

"Yeah, I wanted to upgrade her before I left for college, but she refused," he laughed, leaning against the counter. "Crazy, but I think I understand how this works now. I'll have to come in early and look it over tomorrow before we open."

"When did you go to college?" she asked, knowing he was a few years older than her. He seemed vaguely familiar, but she couldn't place him, those brown eyes ringing all her bells.

"Oh, I left for California several years ago," he said, glancing up at the picture of him in his graduation robe on the desk. "That's me, right there."

"I knew I'd seen you before," she admitted, becoming excited. "You were a few years ahead of me in school, but you'd spend every weekend and most weekdays after school here, right?"

"Yeah, that was me," he said. "I was the oldest, so to escape my siblings, I came here."

"Awesome, I'm an only child, so I never had that problem," Brandi shrugged.

"Oh, that's right; I remember granny would always talk about you when we had new book orders," he said, pointing at the shelf and aisle right in front of them. "You'd sit right down there, and granny would constantly check on you, ensuring you had what you needed."

"What have you been up to since then?" she asked, feeling a bit embarrassed by her girlish escapades that he probably remembered.

The two of them talked for the next hour about his studies in California and his travels to Oregon, Washington, Vancouver, and Mexico. He explained his love for history and the perception people have of it. She found it so intriguing that she had ignored more than one buzz from the phone in her pocket. She was enamored by his thoughts, his way of speaking, and his life that she didn't realize her mouth had fallen open slightly.

"To be honest," Chris spoke, looking shy, "I've been struggling to settle back into town and the library. Granny hasn't made many changes, and she's got to upgrade if she hopes to get state funds and grants for this library to expand and continue."

"I've tried telling her that!" Brandi exclaimed, both of them laughing. "I really have; I've even helped her look up some options on their resource website."

"And?"

"She's not a modern woman," Brandi suggested, shrugging. "So, we're just going to have to help her."

"Oh?" he asked, looking surprised. "What do you mean by that?"

"You upgrade the systems, and then you teach me how to run them," she insisted, pointing at the computer. "I'll take what you teach me and boil it down for granny in a way that will work for everyone."

"You can do that?" he asked, a hint of curiosity in his voice.

"I do it all the time for toddlers; I can do it for your granny," she laughed, squeezing his arm. "How about this weekend, you teach me, and I'll devise a way to teach your granny?"

"Deal," he said, pointing around. "I'd be glad to have the help."

"So, this Saturday? Nine too early?"

"Perfect," he agreed, handing her bag of books to her again. "Have a good night. I'm going to close up and get some dinner."

"Oh, try Rochelle's," she said, pointing out the window. "It's delicious."

"I remember," he said, waving at her as she walked through the door with her purse and bag of books.

Once outside, she giggled happily, excited to return Saturday to see the bright-eyed, dark-haired hunk in those irresistibly sexy glasses. He was something different, someone fascinating, and perhaps, she hoped, her shot at romance in this small, usually quiet town. She found Chris interesting and respected his perspective, studies, and research on his chosen subjects, willing to admit that it was still above her head. She didn't care; she was captivated by his words and the way he explained usually complex ideas.

He was more than attractive, Brandi thought, sitting in her car as she checked her text messages. It was the group text between Joanne, Nevaeh, Courtney, and her. They were talking about some sort of party over the weekend, but Brandi didn't care. She told them she was headed home from the library to shower, eat, and head to bed. However, what she was probably going to do was read the first few chapters of one of her books, stay up too late, and barely make it to work on time the next morning.

CHAPTER FIVE

Chris was walking up the sidewalk, mind full of the kind, beautiful woman from the library the night before. He was headed to his granny's house that morning to check on her before opening the library. He stopped at Roasted Beans Coffee Spot on the way, hiking up the slight hill to overlook the downtown area before heading across the field to his granny's small residential street.

Once he got to the sidewalk, he strode up to his granny's porch and knocked on the door. To his surprise, he heard scrambling inside and some sort of clumsy movement that both frightened and alarmed him. He was about to knock again or force his way through the door, but he heard the lock on the door disengaging, and it opened jerkily.

"Oh!" his grandmother exclaimed, her backbone stiffing upon seeing him. "Christopher, how nice it is for you to come to visit me."

She was wrapped in a blanket, her curly salt and peppered hair bouncing atop her head. She sprung a grin, fiddling with the blanket clenched over what appeared to be a blue jogging suit. She looked slightly distracted, her freckled light brown skin dotted with what looked like flour under her eyes.

"You all right, granny?" he asked, peering past her as he wrapped an arm around her in a hug. She coughed loudly and dryly before letting him in, shutting the door behind him.

"I'm sick; I haven't been out of bed today." She shrugged, moving to the front room where her armchair and chaise couch sat near a small wood stove. Her television, an older flat screen, sat across from them on a small table, leaving the view of the front yard open.

"I smell food," he commented, noticing the flour-covered kitchen counter. The butter and bread smell unmistakable. "I thought you hadn't been out of bed today?"

"Oh," she jumped, looking a bit startled before shaking her head. "No, um, Mabel came by and did that for me. Can you believe it? Wasn't that sweet of her?"

Chris said, agreeing with her. "That was very nice of her, granny."

He wasn't sure what was going on, but his granny's behavior seemed odd. She looked flushed, and her voice wasn't hoarse, but she seemed to be sweaty and a bit jumpy.

"What symptoms do you have?" he asked, sitting across from her.

"Oh, just a slight fever and a sore throat," she said, clearing her throat a few times. "I'll be fine; I just need some rest."

"Any other symptoms? Sweating? Dizziness? Loss of taste? Fatigue?" he was concerned, hoping it wasn't the flu or worse. "I just want to be sure it isn't more serious."

"Oh, no, dear, I'll be all right." She smiled. "How's the library? Anything interesting happen since I've been gone?"

"What?"

"How's it going at the library? Is everything good? Did the plumber come in to take care of that bathroom?"

"Yeah, he'll be there today," Chris said, admiring his granny's slick maneuver to change the subject. "But that computer system is ridiculous."

"What do you mean?"

"I had a misunderstanding with a patron, and I felt awful and looked like an idiot, too," he shrugged and gave a half-smile. "I told you they needed updating; why didn't you let someone do it?"

"I did, but I didn't understand it." She shrugged, hugging the blanket around her tighter.

"You cold?" he asked, his voice low.

"No, I'm just not properly dressed," she snapped, shaking her head. He lowered his brows in confusion, clearly seeing her jogging suit peeking from beneath the blanket. "Who was it? The patron?"

"Oh, Brandi Astore," he said, watching as her eyebrows raised expectantly. "I tried to charge her for fees she didn't owe. It was a mess, but I was glad to see her again. I remember her always coming by the library when I was a child. I haven't seen her in years, and she's changed a lot."

"She's not the same girl she was; I'll admit," his granny sighed. "But she's always been an old soul, a quiet only child."

"I can't imagine…."

"No, no, you can't," she replied. "But she's a good girl, and I'm glad you met her. When you're not around, she's my helper."

"She's pretty smart and very pretty," he replied without thought before realizing his slip and feeling heat creep up his neck. His grandmother chuckled.

"She's too good for a smart mouth like you," she scoffed laughingly, shaking her head. "She's a good girl who deserves a bit of romance."

"I can do romance," he muttered, making her smile. "I'm a master of romance."

"You young'uns don't know a thing about romance," she sighed, glancing at the coffee he still held.

"She does appreciate romance, considering her reading list," Chris said. He felt a bit more embarrassed now, realizing he'd probably seen one of the most private things about Brandi.

Everly smiled at his embarrassment, causing Chris to clear his throat tersely. She chuckled at this, shaking her head before glancing at the clock. It was twenty minutes to nine, and he still had to open the library. She stood now, waving for him to get going and instructing him to leave the coffee. He did so happily, bringing her a simple vanilla latte. She told him she appreciated it, hugged him, and then herded him to the door.

"I'm going to get back to bed, so come back tomorrow, dear," she insisted, opening the door and slightly pushing him out. "Have a good day! Tell your momma I said I'll be over for Sunday dinner."

"Even if you're sick?"

"I'll be fine by then," she said, waving as he walked down the front porch steps and closed the door with a hurried slam. He walked slowly down the block, thinking about his granny's actions, realizing something was off. He decided to follow his intuition. Turning around, he decided to duck behind a hedgerow and a large tree on the corner. He hid there a minute, watching his granny's house. After just a short while, he saw his granny's power-walking friends torpedoing down the road.

They marched right up to his granny's door and knocked. He was in disbelief as he watched her stick her head out the door and look around as if she was in some old sitcom or cartoon. She said something to the group as she emerged onto her porch. She had small weights in her hand and blended right in with the pack of about seven women who began power-walking his way; they all wore the same blue jogging suit that his grandmother had on. She kept up, smiling, chatting, and laughing as they approached. Standing behind the bush, he stood perfectly still and quiet as he watched them disappear down the block toward the school. She didn't even look tired or sick, the mystery becoming that much more irresistible.

What was she up to, and why was she pretending to be sick? There had to be a reason, and he was going to find out. He also knew the perfect person to employ in this adventure. If anything, his granny might be more honest if he had backup.

CHAPTER SIX

oasted Beans Coffee Spot was a bit busy, Joanne flitting happily between tables, the counter, and the storeroom. Her baristas cheerfully brewed, mixed, and handled the rush of customers, but it was clear Joanne needed more employees for busy weekday afternoons. It was a typical day, nothing out of the ordinary, and Brandi was eager to meet Courtney and Neveah at Joanne's as they did weekly for a long lunch. The three of them went to sit on one of the empty couches in the corner.

The place smelled of fresh coffee, vanilla, and cinnamon, and Brandi appreciated it, snuggling into the warmth of the couch between her two talkative friends. They made it a point to come to the café once a week for a long lunch, usually falling on the days Brandi had the good sense to do lunch, playtime, and nap time. Her caregivers and the volunteer moms who stopped in during their lunches to play or eat with their little ones always gave Brandi ninety minutes to enjoy her lunch and coffee.

Joanne was working hard, stopping by the table to write down their needs. When she returned, she stayed a bit, perching herself on the couch arm while her waitress and two baristas made the last few drinks of the rush. She had their preferred beverages in hand, including a cocoa, a cold brew, a latte with far too much espresso, and her own simple cappuccino.

"Busy lunch rush," Joanne smirked, waving for her college-aged waitress to clear the nearby newly vacant table. "It's so nice to have consistent business and loyal customers, but I'm swamped."

"Sounds like you need some more employees," Courtney said, nudging her friend as she sipped her drink.

"I really do," Joanne admitted, thanking the waitress for wiping down the table. "I love the five I have now, but three of them are college students only looking for part-time, so I think one more full-time employee, or maybe two, would really help me out."

"This is your busiest location, Jo," Neveah said, almost knocking over the fake plant on the shelf beside her. She caught it quickly, grimacing at them all as they smiled. "I mean, you should find a local who is willing to learn or maybe advertise online. Do interviews?"

"I was considering that, yeah," Joanne said, Courtney leaning back into the couch comfortably as the soft, jazzy music played over the speakers. The cozy but quirky café had always been a favorite place for the group. It was Joanne's first location where they'd made many happy memories. "If I had three full-time employees, they could all work two full days a week and then take the rest of the week and split it up amongst them and the part-timers."

"You could get rid of a part-timer," Courtney affirmed, glancing at the waitress who had just finished cleaning up another table.

"I don't know if I could do that," Joanne replied, shaking her head. "I like them all, and they're only here for another year or two."

"Fair point, but a full-time employee would be a lot of help." Neveah smiled, foam on her lip.

"Excuse me, miss," a customer at the next table over asked. "Can I get a refill? I see your waitress is busy taking some orders, so, no rush…."

"Oh, not a problem at all, sweety," Joanne said, standing swiftly. "I'll be back after a while, girls. What can I get you? Latte?" she asked the customer, who confirmed.

Joanne hurried off with the customer's cup, happy to refill the order, while her waitress took a four-drink order from a group of students who showed up. Neveah just laughed, sipping her drink as Courtney turned curiously to Brandi.

"Why so quiet?" she asked as Brandi smiled serenely.

"Enjoying myself," Brandi shrugged, sitting her cup down on the table. "Happy to enjoy some adult conversation. Work has been so tiring lately…."

"I know how you feel," Courtney said curtly, Neveah looking up at her, a bit startled.

"What's up at work?" Neveah asked, pressing her for more answers.

"Nothing is going on; it just isn't a very satisfying job." She shrugged, looking out the window now. "It's steady work, which I'm grateful for, but it isn't something I can be passionate about. So I don't even want to show up half the time, and I think my boss knows it."

There was a clatter, Neveah knocking over her mostly empty cup, a bit of liquid spilling over the table and onto the floor. The three women scrambled to clean it up, chuckling and chatting as Neveah went to grab a wet towel from Joanne. She almost tripped over a chair leg, then her own feet, and she bumped into a customer before returning, apologizing profusely.

"Are you sure you need any more espresso?" Courtney asked once the three were comfortably back on the couch.

"I know, I know, but it doesn't make me jittery, and I need the energy," Nevaeh explained, checking her phone quickly. "I've got a meeting with a client, and then I have to go see my boss near Atlanta."

"Wow, when do you have to do that?" Brandi asked, wondering how she would get there and back through the ridiculous amount of traffic after five on weekdays.

"It's not in Atlanta, thankfully, but it is just outside, in some restaurant or bar or something." She shrugged. "I hope he's not trying to hit on me because nothing is happening there, regardless of how rich he is."

The three laughed, giggling about her wealthy and newly single boss, whose last relationship was full of drama. Then Courtney's phone rang, and the three of them paused as she checked it. Joanne had come back to join them; the customers at the counter were mostly gone, and only a few other small groups or single customers with laptops remained.

"What's going on?" Joanne asked Courtney standing and holding up her finger for them to wait.

"My boss, I'll be right back," she whispered, walking to the door and stepping outside onto the sidewalk.

"Wonder what that's about?" Neveah asked, the three of them watching her closely as she spoke on the phone outside.

She was pacing, speaking quickly, and her face was a mixture of stone-cold annoyance and disappointment. She had to know they were watching her, turning to lean against the window as she spoke. The three smirked at this, Joanne propping herself on the sofa next to them as they watched.

"She did say she wasn't satisfied at work," Brandi said, filling Joanne in. "No passion, doesn't want to show up half the time...."

"I can't even imagine," Joanne admitted, looking between them sorrowfully. "I love my job."

"And I love mine." Brandi smiled, Neveah shrugging.

"I love the perks, and I love having clients," Neveah said, siping the fresh cup of plain black coffee that Joanne had brought over. "The pay is great too… but I can't say I am passionate about my job like you two are."

"Do you think Courtney will quit?" Joanne asked, sipping on her bottle of water.

"Don't know, but here she comes." Brandi smiled, the three staring at Courtney as she returned inside.

"Like I said, my job just isn't my passion, and days like today are when I really hate it," Courtney sighed, sitting on the arm of the couch as Joanne wrapped an arm around her in a hug.

"You need a break," Joanne smiled, hugging her closer. "Or a new career… ever consider being a barista?"

"I do love coffee, but I don't think I could find passion in it," Courtney admitted, a frown on her pretty face. "But I appreciate the offer. I just need something more creative that lets me do what I love without making me feel ashamed."

"Ashamed?" Neveah questioned; her eyes were once again wide. "Who is making you feel ashamed?"

"Every time I suggest a creative or unique solution to a problem or offer to work on one of the accounts that require a creative refresh, my boss just shuts me down," she said, her voice full of frustration. "He puts himself on the account, ignores me, or outright shuts me down without even allowing me to show him what I can do. I'm an artist, not just a file on his desk, and it makes me so angry."

"Why would you work for someone like that?" Joanne asked, sounding a little judgmental.

"Well, some of us are grateful for work that's related to what we trained and studied for," Neveah shot back, both she and Joanne locking eyes.

"Settle down, you two," Brandi warned, her voice soft. Those two were always bumping heads. "Courtney can make up her own mind."

"I don't dislike the work," Courtney explained, placing the heels of her palms on her temples and massaging. She was clearly frustrated by the phone call, and the three of them knew she would snap if she didn't make some changes. "But I'd like to be involved in projects that actually challenge me as an artist. I need that passion in my life!"

"We all need a little passion in our lives," Joanne said, hugging her tightly. "Which reminds me… have any of you seen the new librarian?"

"New librarian?" Neveah asked, both she and Courtney listening intently.

"I met him when he came in for coffee," Joanne explained, her voice low. "We chatted a bit, and then I remembered that he used to live here a long time ago. He was a little older than us in school, but his grandmother is Mrs. Everly, the current librarian. She's out sick, so he's stepping in for her."

"He came back here to step in for his sick grandma?" Neveah asked.

"His name is Chris, you remember. Tall, always had that messy head of hair and his nose in a book," Joanne nudged, smiling at Brandi. "He was a senior the year before we entered high school."

"Vaguely," Courtney shrugged, smirking at her. "What about him?"

"He's kind of fine now," Joanne shrugged, making them all giggle. However, Brandi couldn't stop the heat that had flooded her face. She had been thinking the same thing ever since she met him at the library earlier that week. The girls immediately noticed, three sets of eyes honing in on Brandi's reaction.

"Did something happen between our sexy new librarian and our local bookworm?" Courtney asked, her mood completely changed. "We should have known you already met him… spill the details!"

"Agreed," Joanne and Neveah replied, smirking at her.

"There was a misunderstanding, is all," Brandi replied, trying to be more practical than her friends. "He didn't know how to run the old system and thought I owed fees for my books. I didn't and offered to show him how the system worked this Saturday."

"A private training session?" Neveah smirked, she and Joanne giggling.

"Of course, Brandi would call dibs on the hot new librarian," Courtney laughed, hugging her. "Congrats, you'll have to tell us everything Saturday night."

"Nothing is going to happen," Brandi dismissed. "We don't even know each other."

"But you hope something will happen?" Neveah asked, the other two girls encouraging her.

"Maybe, I don't know," Brandi shrugged, feeling embarrassed. "I'm just going to see what happens. We don't even know if we're compatible, and I'd rather wait for him to make the first move if you don't mind."

"Old fashioned, but I like it," Neveah admitted, hugging Brandi with a smile. "Make him come to you, girl."

"You say he's covering for Mrs. Everly? She sure can power-walk for someone who is sick," Courtney said, shaking her head. "I've seen her little club of old ladies march past my office every day, chipper as ever."

"I ran into her at the grocery store the other day," Nevaeh added. "She was smiling and mentioned she'd be going to the senior center for salsa class that night."

"That's so odd; Chris insisted she was sick and contagious," Joanne replied.

Brandi just nodded, sinking into her thoughts as the others continued to converse about Mrs. Everly. She was stuck in her own thoughts about Chris, Mrs. Everly, and her involvement with them both. Brandi was wondering about how weird the whole thing was. It was a bit odd, but what worried her more was that one of her favorite people in the whole world was sick and still acting as if she were fine. Had there been something more serious going on that Chris and Mrs. Everly wanted to hide?

It bothered her as she sat between her friends, who were still discussing Chris and how good-looking he was, his grandma, and some local gossip about a wedding on the horizon between a certain ranger and hairdresser. Brandi had to swim back to the surface now, putting in the effort to let it go and not dwell, eventually deciding that whatever was going on with Mrs. Everly was her own business. Brandi mused that maybe it was a sickness that would come and go. Perhaps it left Mrs. Everly well enough to do some activities, but she couldn't make it through a whole day at the library. It was a logical explanation, as Mrs. Everly wasn't getting any younger.

"Brandi?" Joanne called, standing up. "Hello?"

"Sorry, I was sending some positive thoughts Mrs. Everly's way," she admitted. She was more anxious than ever about Saturday's meeting with Chris and needed to know more.

"Thinking about your library date?" Nevaeh smiled, setting down her empty cup with a clumsy clack.

"I'm hopeful, but I'm not going to invest much of my thought into Chris since it's not like anything happened," Brandi affirmed. "I'm only hoping Mrs. Everly recovers and that he might tell me the truth if I let him know how much I care for her. How much we all do…."

"You think he's lying?" Courtney asked, sounding a bit shocked.

"Either him or Mrs. Everly… but something doesn't add up."

"Don't get ahead of yourself," Joanne warned. "It might be something they just don't want to talk about, Brandi. But, we will all have to accept it if that's their decision."

"True, but I hope it isn't anything like that," Brandi said. The three looked worried, but Brandi knew they had her best interest at heart. She just hoped that seeing Chris Saturday went well. She wasn't going to expect immediate romance just because they both enjoyed the library. Brandi might have been a romantic, but she was also a realist.

CHAPTER SEVEN

The library was quiet and dim when he arrived, locking the doors behind him and switching on the office lights. The rest of the library remained hazed in shadow as Chris went about the daily routine of opening the library and booting up the office equipment, computer lab desktops, and organizing the inbox of books left overnight. He also checked the bathrooms, reorganized the influx of books from the bin, and reshelved them before having his first sip of delicious coffee from Roasted Beans Coffee Spot.

The library would officially open at nine o'clock, and he remained there on weekdays, with an hour-long lunch at one, until dusk, around eight that evening. He had done this already for almost a week, and waves of nostalgia and happiness seemed to wash over him every day. Despite the continued computer troubles, the weekday mornings were mostly quiet. A few older women came in, some retirees met in the library gardens for some chess and checkers, and at noon, the usual group of parents and small children came in for story time, which Chris regarded as his favorite part of the day.

Usually, they'd be reading a couple of classic favorites of his:

The Cat in The Hat and *Oh, the Places You'll Go!* The children loved it when he read Dr. Seuss, and he noticed that the mothers also enjoyed it, giving them time to sit back in the corners and play on their phones. Most of them were kind women, enjoying their half-hour of peace at lunch before thanking him kindly for his reading. It seemed a bit much, the mothers smiling, flirting, and enjoying his company, and he almost had to lock them out at one, so he could enjoy his lunch in peace.

Today, however, on this nice Saturday, everything seemed to be busy right from the start. After officially opening the doors, groups of locals came streaming in. Soon the library computer lab, gardens, and lounge were buzzing with people, all browsing, chatting, and being extremely loud for a library setting. He spotted Rochelle from the diner, Mrs. Zhang close behind, as well as several other faces from his grandmother's circle. It hadn't been an hour, and already he'd checked out a dozen books and set three people up with new library cards. Unfortunately, the computer system was still being a pain, so Chris did what his grandmother had always taught him – when in doubt, follow your instincts.

So, starting with the first library customer, he'd written and stamped out the books the old-fashioned way, handing them a copy slip of the return date for the book and a signature. He was doing just this for the last person in line almost an hour later when a familiar face came through the door. It was his best friend, Nate, who went for a run every Saturday morning. This morning, it seemed he wanted to stop in and visit. However, he was quickly approached by several people in the community, all delighted to see him and talk to him about everything and anything.

"I've been well, Mrs. Zhang, working on helping Mr. Knight upgrade his tech so he can handle more orders," Nate explained, smiling at another familiar face, who offered him a hug.

"You've been so busy, Nate," an older woman commented, a few of the others gathering around to greet him. "You think you could help Niles with his computer issues? He's having a hard time upgrading his sales system online, you see...."

"Not a problem; I'll stop over on my run after I leave here," he assured, hugging another person he knew.

"You think you could have a look at my social pages?" a local hairdresser asked, a friendly smile on her face.

"Not a problem; send me links online, and I'll be happy to see what we can do to monetize your content," he said, noticing Chris watching him.

"Don't forget to stop by for some lunch later, on the house, for helping me with my website," Rochelle insisted, Mrs. Zhang waving at him as he made his way toward the desk and Chris.

"Not a problem. I'm sure I'll see you all at the upcoming festival, and there is a council meeting coming up, so I hope to see you all there as well," he said, waving casually as he finally made his way up to the desk.

"Popular as usual," Chris smirked, sorting through some books on the desk before peeking into the computer lab at a couple of pre-teens playing some sort of block game. "How's it going?"

"It's going; been busy all week, really." Nate shrugged, looking at the slowly thinning library crowd. "How about you? How's granny doing? Still sick?"

"That's unclear, but I'll tell you more about that later," Chris smirked, glancing around to ensure they weren't overheard. "I met a beautiful woman a few days ago, and she'll be stopping in today to help me with this outdated computer system."

"Oooooh," he drawled, leaning in closer, his dark eyes twinkling as he rubbed his hand across his low-cut fade. "Who? I've lived here a long time, my friend, and there isn't a beautiful woman I haven't noticed...."

"Brandi Astore, you know her?"

"The name isn't familiar, but I have undoubtedly seen her if she is as attractive as you say." Nate shrugged, glancing around.

"I'll bet you have." Chris chuckled, shoving him slightly as they exchanged hushed words. "You seem to know everybody in this town."

"Well, when your dad has been the mayor since you were in middle school, it makes it impossible not to," Nate retorted, smiling at a pretty woman browsing the romance section.

"You do know that your dad is the mayor, right? Not you?"

"That's not why I stopped by, you know." Nate winked, glancing over his shoulder toward the nearest group of browsers. "You're coming to my party, right?"

"Of course, I told you I was, didn't I?" Chris asked, smiling kindly at a passing patron.

"Good, because you need to relax, let off some steam," he said, the jingling bell of the front doors catching both of their attention.

Chris froze in that moment, Brandi walking through the door in a long mustard yellow and patterned flower dress, her boots up to her knees. Her bright eyes seemed to twinkle in the streaming sunshine from the window, and Nate had to stop himself from shaking Chris out of his daze.

"That's her," Chris said, waving at her as she approached, her smile wide and dimpled.

"I've seen her around," Nate whispered back, waving at her too. "Pretty, but a bit too bookish for me. Definitely your type...."

"Hello," Brandi said, stopping at the desk now. "How has it been going this morning?"

"A bit busy," Chris admitted, watching her peer around at the familiar faces, waving at some.

"I'm Nate, by the way." Nate smiled, holding out his hand officially. "I've seen you around town many times, but I don't think we've been introduced."

"Oh, I know you," she affirmed, politely shaking his hand. "I've lived here my whole life, so I can definitely recognize the mayor's son. I'm Brandi. And aren't you also India's boyfriend? I've seen you together a few times."

"Nice to meet you, Brandi," he said, looking a bit uncomfortable, turning back to Chris. "But I've got to head out. I've got some businesses to stop by and some people to talk to before heading back to the office."

"I'll text later," Chris assured, noticing Brandi narrowing her eyes at the way Nate avoided her question. She came around the counter, wishing him a good day.

"It was nice meeting you, Brandi," Nate smiled sheepishly, waving back at her. "See you around."

"You, too," she called after him with a suspicious look on her face.

"So, I've been just keeping manual copies of books that have been checked out today," Chris explained, pointing to the organized stack of receipts. "And I haven't officially checked in the books that were left in the overnight bin, but they definitely aren't late."

"Not a problem, but first things first." She smiled, slipping off her long dark shawl. "I'll show you how to check them in on the old system."

Chris was grateful that she showed him this, watching closely as she typed in the information needed to input the book back into the digital system. It was a bit protracted and repetitive, but without the proper program, the scanner his grandmother needed was useless for checking the books in and out. A few times, as she explained the system, he interrupted her, showing her a quicker way to input the numbers and borrower information. He also wanted to correct her about the proper order to organize the files, but she patiently explained to him why he was wrong.

He didn't like that, insisting that it'd be much more efficient to look up the book by title instead of author. However, instead of correcting him, she allowed him to do so, which turned out to be an utter disaster. She never once judged him, though, and never said I told you so, and even though Chris complained about the system being outdated and that he knew better, she stayed patient and helpful. Unfortunately, his organizational method in the program only made it that much harder, still sorting the book by author and putting his updated title in a file totally unrelated to the genre or author.

He knew better than this, was taught better than this, and hated looking like an idiot in front of this clearly smart and beautiful woman. However, it wasn't in his nature to be wrong, as he knew everything there was to know about the library sciences. He had made it a point to study the old and new systems as well as the upgraded methods of loaning books through other libraries. However, none of that mattered here when the system was almost thirty years out of date.

His frustration melted away as he finally stopped questioning her methods and followed her logic and the system's rules. By their lunch break, he was completely comfortable inputting the information his grandmother's way. He was also more at ease following Brandi's lead, something that was new to him as he'd always been the one to know exactly what needed to be done. He'd never really been a follower, except maybe of his parents and grandmother, and felt awkward when Brandi insisted she take the lead and help him. That afternoon, the library was busier than usual, both working together to keep up with the returns and check-outs. She even showed him a quick keyboard shortcut to find specific titles by author. Of course, the authors were in alphabetical order, but the titles were in release order, something he disliked very much.

However, none of that mattered as she showed him how to find library card numbers without having to leave the checkout screen. This made everything much faster for him, and he thanked her multiple times, willing to admit that she clearly knew more about this library and its systems than he had given her credit for. It wasn't until after four that it started to die down; people beginning to clear out almost an hour before the library's closing at six on Saturdays.

This was the perfect opportunity for them to chat, clean up, and hopefully get to know one another. Chris had wanted this all day, seeing her flit around the library with patrons and books like some sort of magician.

"Busy day," Chris commented, putting the last of the returns back on the shelf in the romance section.

"It was, but I love those kinds of days, if I'm honest," she admitted, popping around the corner with the last of her returns. "People coming to the local library makes me happier than I can possibly explain."

"Same," he admitted, his smile wide. "Seeing curious faces, excited hands reaching out for books, and illuminated eyes while they're reading from the pages is a real rush."

"I can agree with that," she breathed, placing her last book on the shelf. "There is something about being in the presence of books, isn't there?"

"Absolutely, like its own brand of magic," Chris affirmed, following her back to the desk. "But that's why I love history too. It's a magic that we can confirm, you know? Like a science, testing theories and using technology to find the truth of a past long forgotten... it's exhilarating, really."

"I get that, though I can't say that my passion is history," she admitted, smiling widely, pushing her hair back over her ear. "My passion is more... passion."

They both chuckled at this, Brandi stacking the last of the library newsletters on the counter as Chris leaned against it. Brandi blushed as he looked intently at her, the both of them moving to a couple of the lounge chairs near the reading nook. The library was mostly empty, so it wouldn't hurt for them to relax and chat for a while. Chris might have been a bit uptight when it came to his organization system, but he wasn't opposed to a casual conversation on the clock.

"So, you went to school out west, right?" Brandi asked, crossing her legs in the oversized comfortable chair.

"Yeah, I went to school in San Francisco and then got my Masters in Pasadena," he explained, sitting in the chair next to her. "I wasn't sure what I wanted to do with my life, but I'm glad I chose what I did. I hope to one day write a book, but for now, I enjoy studying history."

"That's so adventurous." Brandi smiled, resting her hands in her lap. "I've wanted to see the world, but I'm so in love with my job, and I couldn't possibly consider leaving my children."

"Oh, you have children?" Chris asked, eyes wide.

"Oh no, I'm the director and head teacher at the daycare downtown," she said with pride. "I love my job so much.

"I envy that," he admitted, rubbing the back of his neck. "I just came back from California because I've finished my dissertation."

"Do you know what you want to do next?" she asked, tucking her feet under her thighs. "I mean, now that you've finished your studies?"

"To be honest, I'm not sure." He smiled, leaning his head against the palm of his hand as he lounged in the chair. "I was planning on applying for some academia or museum positions, but coming back here has made me miss home more than ever. I don't know if I'm ready to leave Sweetgum again."

"Ah, you've fallen back in love," she said, sighing contently. "Sweetgum has that effect on its children, doesn't it? But as they say, there really is no place like home."

"I've been thinking about that more and more," Chris replied, nodding his affirmation. "I mean, not just home but finding my place, you know?"

"I understand that in many ways," she said, her eyes widening. "My children often ask me hard questions, and sometimes it's impossible to come up with elegant answers. Toddlers are so inquisitive and fascinating to observe and are always observing us. They can be persistent; however, there's always a method I like to apply that gets them thinking about their own thoughts, their own path."

"Yeah?"

"What is it you want more than anything?" she asked, her eyes alight. "And their eyes and thoughts just flood out like a wave. It's beautiful to behold...."

Chris listened to her speak about the children as her eyes glistened beautifully in the light. Even as they started putting away books, equipment, and shutting down computers, all Chris could think about was how natural she was. It was obvious she loved her job and those children. It was also apparent that she was destined to work with them, to light their emerging minds with flames of curiosity. He loved that so much and admired her every move as they talked and walked about the library checking everything one last time.

"I wish I was as sure as you. I'm not sure if I want to settle down here or not," Chris finally admitted, locking the back door of the library. "I really admire that you know exactly what you want to do in life. I wish I knew myself that well. But, unfortunately, here I am with a Ph.D. dissertation and no plan."

"Don't be silly," she breathed, stopping him as the lights in the library switched off, leaving the glow of only the office lamps and streetlights outside. "Sometimes those moments when we don't have a plan become our most important milestones of self-discovery."

Chris was drawn into her deep eyes, bright and beautiful in the glow of golden light. She was smiling, encouraging him to dig deep, and he was so enamored by her beauty that he hardly thought of what he'd said at all. It didn't matter. The two of them were only inches apart, standing in the entry to the library's office. He saw her eyes fall bashfully as she realized what was happening. Brandi had the sense to step back, regaining herself with a sigh and glancing at the clock above them.

"Well, I should be going," she said, grabbing her purse from the shelf inside the office door. "Do you have it from here?"

"Yeah, I can set the alarm and lock up." He smiled, his face flushed at how she bit her bottom lip. He was glad that his complexion made it hard to detect. Brandi hoisted her purse over her shoulder tightly, grabbing up her shawl to wrap around her.

"You're welcome to come back anytime to help out," he told her before she reached the door. "Or if you just want to hang out."

She turned and smiled at him over her shoulder, her eyes twinkling. He couldn't help but smile back stupidly, unable to stop himself from just looking at her. She was so pretty and sweet.

"I could always use the company," he continued, unable to stop himself. "And you seem to be here a lot anyway...."

"All right, if nothing comes up, I'll be back to help next Saturday." She smiled, waving at him. "I'll see you soon."

With that, she was gone; Chris felt positively stupid five minutes later when he realized he was still smiling. It was time to close up, and he was ready to leave, but for some reason, he couldn't get rid of the ache in his cheeks from the smiling. He also couldn't ignore the ache in his heart that Brandi had created when he left.

CHAPTER EIGHT

Monday morning was an early one for Brandi, arriving at work before the others to open and prep breakfast. When Lehna, Shea, and Alyza arrived a half hour later with coffees, she was ecstatic. However, all three of them were immediately curious about her weekend date at the library, which she divulged reluctantly. She was never one to kiss and tell, but truthfully, they hadn't kissed. Quite honestly, she wasn't sure if she wanted to if he wasn't going to be staying in Sweetgum.

"So, tell us everything before the first drop-off," Shea demanded, smirking at her playfully. "How was it?"

"Yes, I need the details. My weekend was so boring," Alyza hummed, pulling her hair up into a messy bun and headband.

"Well, it wasn't that exciting, really," Brandi explained, telling them about the computer system, what they talked about, and how busy it was. It wasn't that exhilarating, but Brandi had thought about it the rest of the weekend and all morning. Something about it made her buzz, giving her a giddy feeling of anticipation that she absolutely loved about her favorite novels.

"You need to just go up to him and ask for a date," Shea said, unlocking the front doors.

"No, no, he needs to come to you," Alyza replied, shaking her head. She was checking the food trays and drinks. "He needs to ask you out on a proper date. You need to wear something sexy, suggest a date, and he'll be drawn to you like honey."

"She doesn't need to be that obvious, but she does need to know her worth," Lehna commented, making them all nod their approval. "He can ask you, but if he doesn't, you should take the chance and ask him."

"Firstly, I don't even know if he's interested," Brandi replied, waving them off. "And if he is, I doubt he'll stay in Sweetgum long, anyway."

"Nonsense, for love he would stay," Shea professed, making Brandi smile at her certainty.

However, her mind was dwelling on the idea of Chris leaving and finding a life somewhere else. She knew it would be selfish to want him to stay, and really they didn't even know each other that well. She was probably overthinking it. She loved her life here and felt she was only missing someone she could love. Perhaps she was too romantic, but she wanted passion in her life and didn't want to catch feelings for someone who wasn't going to stick around.

As the four of them prepped breakfast, there was a knock at the front doors. They were all a bit shocked and worried, realizing that drop-off didn't start for another half hour. Brandi walked out to the front and was surprised to see Chelsea standing there with her small son.

"Hey Chelsea, what's going on?" Brandi asked, eyes wide. She hoped there wasn't an emergency, but Chelsea just stood there, phone in one hand, her purse over her other shoulder.

"Nothing," Chelsea replied, her eyebrow raised incredulously. "I'm here to drop off my son."

"Oh, well, I'm happy to take him early if there's an emergency," Brandi tried to explain, looking over the little boy cautiously. "But as a general rule, drop off starts at seven-thirty."

"Yeah, okay, that's great," she replied, looking up from her phone again. "Thanks. I'll be back later."

Brandi was furious now, her temper flaring as she watched Chelsea aimlessly stare at her phone again. She didn't even apologize or give an explanation. She also didn't appreciate her flippant way of speaking and interacting with people, like it was beneath her. Brandi did say she could drop him off if it were an emergency, but she wasn't sure how Chelsea took this as a yes. It was also embarrassing that she didn't even treat Brandi with respect as the head of the school.

"Oh, and I forgot to tell you," Chelsea spoke, looking up from her phone. "Grayson eats his lunch early, so feed the children at ten-thirty instead of eleven-thirty, okay?"

Brandi tried her best to put on a smile, painfully glancing at the other three, who stood there angrily, speechless. Brandi, however, had to remain in control and professional, something that was harder than she wanted to admit with this woman. Even her son seemed to realize something was wrong.

"I'm sorry, but that isn't our schedule," Brandi responded tightly. "Our schedule is on the parent portal of our website."

"I'm aware; I saw it," Chelsea responded shortly, her voice full of attitude. "But the schedule I'm giving you makes so much more sense. I'll email you my other thoughts on the class schedule so you can adjust accordingly."

Brandi could feel the anger and outrage rising, never having to deal with a parent so disrespectful and pushy. She didn't know how to set Chelsea straight without being rude, and she still didn't understand how a parent could ignore their child so blatantly. She also didn't know how to respond to such horrible manners.

"No need to thank me." Chelsea waved, smiling down at her son before turning to the door with a laugh. "I'll be back. I will be at the office all day, so if you need to reach me, my email is in your files."

Chelsea left before Brandi could respond, Shea quickly picking up on her baffled expression and helping Grayson to get comfortable in the other room. She offered to give him an orange before breakfast was served while he enjoyed playing with some puzzle games. Brandi, however, needed a moment.

"I'll be right back," she sighed, going to her office and shutting the door. She had no idea how to deal with this parent. Holding her head in her hands, she groaned, wondering how to be more assertive in a respectful manner. She hated for this to escalate, but she knew for a fact that Chelsea was intentionally ignoring her. That was more infuriating than she cared to admit, but she also wondered if something more troublesome was going on in their lives.

CHAPTER NINE

hris was organizing books and cleaning shelves when the library phone rang. Hoisting himself down from one of the taller shelves, he almost sprinted to the phone, catching it on the last ring.

"Sweetgum Library, how may I help you?" Chris asked.

"Hi, I was just wondering if the library ever hosted any events for teens," a female voice asked, her friendly southern accent ringing out over the buzzing line. "My children are on the computer too much for my taste, and I'm looking for community activities they could participate in outside school and the house. Somewhere they can make in-person friends, you know?"

"I understand." Chris smiled, happy to help the woman. "Technology has a way of hypnotizing, but books and libraries had the same effect on me when I was a child."

"Exactly," she replied, sounding excited now. "I think they could benefit from some time outside the home and off the screen."

"Let me see what we've got on our community calendar." Chris smiled, going to the computer. Brandi had taught him how to pull up the library and community calendars, and he was curious about what the library offered. To his surprise, he found a few book sales, some adult author events, and some book club meetings, but nothing in the way of teen events.

"I'm sorry," he said, hearing her sigh over the line. "We don't seem to have any events that would appeal to children or teens. It's quite odd, but I don't see anything besides sales and author events."

"Could you think about starting some?" the woman asked, making Chris pause. "I mean, even some craft ideas, painting, arts, maybe book readings of sorts for the little ones…."

"We do have book readings on weekdays for toddlers," he said, making a note to put those on the calendar. "But I will definitely reach out to you when we come up with more events. Can you leave your contact information for me?"

"Absolutely," she replied, shuffling around. He wrote down her email, phone number, and first name.

"My daughters used to like knitting and making crafts like bracelets and scrapbooking," the woman explained, reaffirming her interest. "A teen book club would be great as well. Reading young adult fiction is all the rage online and off, so I'm told."

"I'll definitely come up with something," he replied, "And let you know."

"Thanks," she replied, wishing him a good day and hanging up.

He thought about the clubs and events he could organize. He knew what he liked, history and tabletop games like Dungeons and Dragons and various wargames, and stubbornly, he didn't want to really go outside his comfort zone. He didn't know anything about knitting, crafts, or similar interests. He liked the familiar to the point of obsession. He wouldn't apologize for being a creature of habit and a consistent organizer. After all, he was the librarian here, at least until his granny decided to come back to work. He was still wary and curious about what she was really up to, but she seemed happy, despite her claims of illness.

By that afternoon, he'd already brainstormed ten different ideas, clubs, and various child-friendly events he could do for the community. He hadn't realized how much he had missed planning his own friends' events and joining campaigns. Even in college, when he didn't have as much time, he enjoyed the camaraderie of in-person gaming. He wondered if children would even be interested in that form of play and wondered how he could find out.

After updating the event calendar online and making a few lists in a new notebook, Chris considered the implementation of the activities. He had his own tabletop games he could use and donate, starting the fascination and interest in board games throughout the community. Knowing how quiet and conservative the town was, he wondered how everyone would feel about it. However, he knew the game and comic shop would have the needed materials.

It would be a major increase in sales and activities for both the comic shop and the library. He had come up with nights he could take on the extra work and perhaps some potential donors and organizations eager to help out the youth and the library. Chris was so deep into his own thoughts and ideas about games, book readings, and releases that he didn't realize his own lunch had come and gone.

He did notice, however, that his usual afternoon reading group had come in and that he had to scarf down bites of sandwich between patrons. They didn't seem to mind, a few older women asking about his grandma and his plans. He liked entertaining them usually, but today he wanted to organize his thoughts and plans for these clubs. He waited for the crowds to die down after three, but it soon picked back up when school activities released, sending a wave of children and teens into the library for the next two hours.

Chris was happy that the rest of the evening was quiet, seeing a few familiar faces return and check out some popular books. He was content to help them and chat a bit, but he was truly engaged in his event planning for the library. Suddenly, he remembered Brandi, excited to see her again that Saturday. Now, he could ask her opinion about the events. After all, she did work with children every day. His excitement and impatience were amplified, and he could feel the buzzing in his stomach over her impending visit to the library.

CHAPTER TEN

*B*randi had wrestled with her conscience and thoughts the rest of that week, questioning whether she should return to the library. She had promised Chris she'd be back Saturday but didn't want to start something that went nowhere. She didn't want to risk heartbreak and disappointment for either of them. However, after wrestling over it all week and waking up early Saturday, she was no closer to what she truly wanted to do.

After a cup of coffee and some jitters, Brandi dressed in a cute dress and put her hair up. She had to return her books either way and if she ended up sticking around to help, so be it. If not, then leaving quickly with her new books would definitely distract her from thoughts of him. After checking her outfit and applying some natural makeup, she was ready to take her bag of books back to the library.

She walked up the block, enjoying the warmth of the February morning, and arrived at the library early, only a half hour after they had opened. There weren't many other patrons there yet, and she found her stomach fluttering when she entered the building. She was surprised to see Chris at the circulation desk sorting through some old boxes of games and random items. She wasn't sure what he was doing, but when he noticed her, he smiled widely, eager to chat.

"I was hoping you'd stop by today," Chris admitted, showing her his stacks of games. "How was your week?"

"A bit dull, but that's all right," she admitted, showing him her bag of returns. "What are you doing?"

"I got a phone call earlier this week about starting up some community events for teens and children," he explained, showing her his notebook. "I wanted to make a list of good ideas, and I decided to start a club for teen tabletop games."

"That sounds really interesting," she admitted, looking over one of the game covers and his opened notebook page. "I've never seen a club like that around here before, but I know it's a great idea to get children and teens involved in the library."

"I wanted to do a set of history screenings, too," he explained, showing her his ideas. "Each week, I would do a different history documentary in the media room and a display of books related to the history in the film just outside."

"I like that; it would get a lot of patrons interested in history," Brandi agreed. "You could do all sorts of history, local or national, well-known or obscure. Either way, it is unique and interesting."

"I thought so too and could probably include a calendar with the newsletter every month," Chris said, jotting down a note in the booklet.

"I'd also consider asking patrons what they'd like," Brandi suggested, motioning at his notebook. "Either ask every teen and child when they come in to write down their ideas in a suggestion box or do an online poll."

"I'm not sure about that," Chris drawled, frowning. "The parents want them to socialize and get away from what they already know. Getting them interested in things they wouldn't normally find interesting...."

"True, but an informal survey might surprise you," she encouraged, smiling softly as she checked in her books. "You could ask for their opinions on subjects they are curious about too."

"That could work, and it would give me more ideas," he said, willing to admit that it wouldn't be successful without the children's support.

"Wait, I know!" Brandi exclaimed, setting aside her books. "Teens can be a bit awkward, so let's make it easy on them. Give me one minute."

With a swirl of her long dark dress, she disappeared into the computer lab. Chris was curious but waited patiently, checking in her books and reshelving a few before she returned. When she did, she popped around the corner of the aisle, waving excitedly at him with a stack of papers under her arm.

"I created a survey," she explained, showing him one of the printed sheets. "Give one of these out to every teen that comes in, and they can put them in the inbox. This way, they can pick from some interesting subjects and give you a bit of insight into their minds. They can write down their interests, choose from various topics, and you can tailor your events around those interests.

"That's brilliant," Chris admits, reading over the few questions. "I like that you ask their favorite genres and their age."

"I just know that you can learn a lot from asking other people questions," Brandi shrugged, squeezing his shoulder. "If you want to create events to serve the community, then you should ask the community questions first."

Chris considered this, realizing he didn't usually ask other people questions. Instead, he usually jumped right into a project or an idea, usually based on his own judgment and knowledge. Chris then considered that this probably resulted from working as an academic, a lone profession that sometimes required solitude. He understood the fundamental principles behind researching characters but never considered applying this to the people in his own life. It was an eye-opening revelation.

The rest of the morning was full of ideas, the day only picking up when a small group of students came in to check out some school-related books. Afterward, Brandi and Chris talked at length about ideas for children-related events. Brandi had a lot of ideas for the younger children, coming up with holiday-themed events as well as summer reading ideas, clubs, and various in-person hobbies to entice young readers into the library.

She even asked several parents' opinions who had stopped in that afternoon, all of them excited for the opportunity to be a part of the new children-friendly program at the library. The parents were kind, encouraging, and honest about what they and their children liked, and Chris was amazed at Brandi's willingness to jot down notes and offer them ideas and suggestions.

The parents of the younger children were very clear and excited about the recent implementation of his story hour for children. Their encouragement was endless, but they also wanted a bit more. One parent suggested a Lego club and another suggested board games like Chris had hoped, which only spurred on their creative process until well after a late lunch ordered from Rochelle's. When the influx of patrons died down, Brandi suggested some community events for the adults as well, something Chris hadn't considered yet.

"I mean, we do live in a small town," she said, motioning to the library around them. "My own book club meets at Rochelle's Diner every week instead of the library, which is a bit strange. Don't get me wrong, I love Mrs. Everly very much, but she's not a big community event lover. I've even told her before that doing events would bring us all together, but she wouldn't budge."

"Ah, yeah, granny can be a bit stubborn," he admitted. "But I love the idea of clubs and more community involvement with the library. It is a great place for people of all ages to gather, so I will definitely pressure granny into considering more events."

"Sounds reasonable." Brandi smiled as she offered to help him shelve some returns and tidy up.

They enjoyed the rest of the day together, sorting books, brainstorming ideas, and interacting with different people in the community. Rochelle came in again, asking about their lunch, and a few more familiar faces from the community center and the local school were also in for specific book requests. While they were sorting the last customers of the weekend, Brandi caught herself thinking of Chris and his plans.

She secretly wished Chris was set on sticking around in Sweetgum for a while. The more time she spent around him, the more she liked him. It seemed like every moment that day was full of excitement and flirting, something she embraced happily. On the other hand, Brandi didn't know if she could explore this connection any further and if he might up and leave the library, and Sweetgum, at any time. These thoughts somewhat overshadowed the rest of their day together, and when Brandi was ready to go, she lingered around to offer Chris an opportunity to ask her out, just like Lehna had suggested.

When he didn't take the bait, she simply smiled, squeezed his arm gently, and picked up her newest books from behind the counter. She'd once again been at the library all day Saturday, and it seemed nothing but flirting, and a bit of disappointment came out of it. Luckily, she had her favorite authors to keep her company on that lonely Saturday night.

CHAPTER ELEVEN

That next day, Chris walked up the street from his mom's house to visit his grandmother. He'd only talked to her on the phone lately and hadn't seen her since the day he spotted her sneaking out with her power-walking group. He was eager to run ideas by her and check on her condition in person. When he got to the front porch, he noticed she had a lot of holiday-themed decorations outside for late winter that was specific to Sweetgum. Her yard items, Sweetgum flags, and décor were packed in boxes on her porch, and it seemed she had planned to decorate that sunny Sunday.

He knocked at the door happily, waiting patiently for any movement or sign that she was approaching the door. When he knocked and rang the bell again, he realized that she wasn't going to answer. So he tried calling her phone, hearing it ring inside before going to the answering machine. He was worried now as his granny only ever used a landline. Thinking the worse, Chris was about to call his mom so she could contact her fire department friends. He had his phone in hand and was worried about his granny's distress when he spotted a familiar group of older women coming down the sidewalk from around the corner.

Thinking quickly, Chris dove behind his granny's car, sliding down the other staircase to crouch behind her old caddy. To his surprise and confusion, granny was walking, talking, smiling, and seemed otherwise healthy as they passed the house on their route around the block. Chris stood silent, hiding until they were out of sight down the street.

Chris didn't know why he was hiding from his grandmother. It wasn't as if he was in the wrong, watching over her while she seemed to walk a marathon with a temperature and some sort of flu. She looked perfectly fine, not even red-faced, as the group passed by at their usual, increasing speed. It irritated Chris the more he thought about it, wondering why his granny would lie to him. He couldn't resist and had to know what was going on, taking off down the driveway and sidewalk after them.

It didn't take too long, the women rounding the corner towards a small community park for children and dogs. He was only a few long strides behind them when one of the older women spotted him over her shoulder. She jumped a bit, looking worried before whispering something to his granny. The others seemed to swarm at this, like watching bees in a hive. Soon, they were all weaving and moving, his granny disappearing amongst them until he could no longer make out her hair or green tracksuit.

He tried to ignore the fact that the group had stopped just shy of a set of tall bushes and shrubs, his granny almost blending in with them as she hid. He didn't call her out on this, instead smiling at the women kindly. He found it a bit funny and ironic that he was the one just hiding from her, and now the roles had reversed. He waved kindly at the group of seven women, who all waved back casually as if nothing was out of the ordinary.

"Good morning, ladies." He smiled, reaching out to hug one of his granny's sisters, whom he affectionately referred to as auntie.

"Sorry to bother you," Chris continued, smiling kindly at some of the unfamiliar faces. "But I was just at granny's, and she won't answer the door. I'm really worried about her and was going to have mom call her firefighter friend to see if we couldn't get inside the house to check on her. I don't suppose any of you ladies have seen or spoken to her today?"

The group shook their head collectively, looking quite guilty as they watched him. He could tell something was off, but he didn't understand why they were doing this. As far as he knew, his granny was content at her job and in life, excited for him to come back home for months now. But when he finally did, she acted as if she was too sickly to even see him. However, here she was, blatantly hiding from him in a bush while he questioned her accomplices.

"Well, I did almost break down her door just now, so maybe something is wrong," he surmised, sounding slightly more panicked. "I think I should just break in and check on her. What do you think, ladies? I could always replace a pane of glass or a broken door handle. You think I should break in, Auntie?"

"No!" his granny shouted, the rest of them scrambling with similar responses. Chris looked between them curiously; his eyebrow raised as he scanned their still sour but sympathetic eyes. Chris, however, was struggling to hold back a laugh at his granny's uncontrollable reaction.

"Who was that?" Chris asked, peering at the bush casually.

"Me, me," said one of the women in the back, clearing her throat. "There's been a bug going around, you know?"

"I do know... that's why I'm worried about granny." He smiled serenely, knowing he'd caught her in a trap. "I think breaking the pane on the door might be my best bet, as I know granny doesn't have a spare key."

"No need for that, sonny," one of the other older women spoke up, taking the lead. "I think Everly told us she had a doctor's appointment today to try and get better medication for this flu. It seems to be burning right through her. Why, just the other day, I dropped off some soup…."

"I made her a casserole, too," another woman smiled, supporting her friend's story.

"So odd that she was able to find a doctor open on a Sunday in Georgia." Chris shrugged, dismissing it. "But that's granny for you. She's always been industrious and slightly pushy. I wouldn't be surprised if she went to visit the doc at his home directly. However, I've had my reservations since I returned."

"What do you mean, Chris?" his auntie asked, smiling kindly.

"I don't know; I have a feeling that there is something else going on with granny," he explained, nodding slowly. "You ladies don't think she's faking it, do you?"

The group went silent, the guilt evident in their eyes and faces, but none of them would betray his granny. Even his aunt, who looked nervous and guilty, didn't break, knowing his granny was listening to their every word. That didn't bother Chris, admiring the closeness that the group had at their age.

"Well, anyway, if you see her, could you have her call me? I need to talk to her about some changes I want to make at the library," Chris continued, hugging his auntie one more time. "Take care of yourself, okay? And get a hold of me if you talk to her, okay? I'm headed to Troy's house for the game. Feel free to stop by and see the children. They've grown so much it's unbelievable."

Chris waved goodbye to them all, kind words called after him as he rounded the corner toward his car. He had parked at his brothers the next block over and was happy to walk there, relieved to see that his brother's wife and their children had just returned from church and were all outside to greet him as he came up the drive. He was happy and pleasantly surprised to see his mother and father there as well, eager to spend time with the children after church every Sunday.

"Was wondering where you wandered off to," his father said, eyeing him curiously. "What's up?"

"Just went to check on granny," Chris admitted, waving politely at his sister-in-law and the young children. "How was service?"

"Long but good," his mother said, waving her fan in her face. "It's a warm winter day that I think we all can appreciate. So who is up for barbeque today?"

"I've got some chicken we can barbeque," Lynnette offered, smiling down at her children. "I stopped at the grocery store yesterday, so they are still in the fridge. Lots of thighs and wings."

"Perfect, I'll run home and grab the potato salad and coleslaw," his mother encouraged, taking his oldest niece's hand. "Come with me, Maya, Christina; we'll go to granny's house and get some goodies before the game starts."

"Be careful!" Lynette called after them, his father eagerly following the group of three down the block toward their home. Chris waved after them and then offered to help his brother Lewis and Lynette prep the kitchen and the grill. While Lynette was inside basting the chicken in buttermilk, Chris and Lewis were outside messing with the barbeque grill. The radio was on in the garage nearby, so they could hear the game's announcers, knowing it hadn't started yet. The day was warm, and the sweet Georgia air gave him a sense of nostalgia he really appreciated.

"What's up?" Lewis asked, noticing his attitude. "You're acting a bit odd today. Something wrong?"

"I think granny is lying about her sickness," Chris replied, smirking at him. "Hear me out."

"I guess, but I don't know why she'd lie about that." Lewis smiled, closing the barbeque lid so it would heat up the coals.

"Maybe granny just needs a break, but she is is still active as ever," Chris explained, carrying some utensils over to the large picnic table under the awning. "Rochelle tells me she's been doing the same power-walking route every morning. Every time I stop by unannounced, she's up and moving around. Grandma doesn't seem sick, but she does seem up to something. She's never asked for help with the library before, so maybe this is her way of getting a break."

"Then I say we give it to her." Lewis smiled, waving at their parents, who had just come through the backyard gate. "She's not harming anyone, and she's old. So let her enjoy some time off, Chris. It won't hurt to stick around at the library for a bit longer, would it, Mr. California?"

Chris bristled, shrugging at the suggestion but agreeing with his brother's logic. He decided that maybe Chris didn't know what granny was up to, but she seemed healthy and wanted him to run the library for now. That was something he could do with a smile on his face because he'd met someone more interesting than he could have possibly imagined and needed to know more. For the rest of the day, throughout the game and the delicious barbeque, all he could think about was Brandi's smiling face and the touch of her soft and caring hand.

CHAPTER TWELVE

Brandi was in her office at the daycare, the girls handling the end-of-the-day routine. After three, the children would play, enjoy some puzzles or games, and enjoy some final outdoor time before pickup. Brandi had been considering how to assert herself with Chelsea all day, distracted by the uncertainty that came with it. She knew that the only way she could deal with Chelsea was to be assertive, and Chelsea did not seem like the kind of woman that took kindly to resistance or criticism. Even if it was for the good of her own child, Brandi doubted Chelsea would hear any of it.

Brandi just couldn't let one parent walk all over her in front of her students, her assistants, and the other parents. It just wasn't how things were done, and Chelsea, even though she was an outsider, should have known better. If Brandi went to wherever she worked and treated her like that, she'd be furious. However, the idea of a conflict or a major meltdown in front of her employees and children was horrifying. She did not doubt that the other parents wouldn't be affected, except that maybe Chelsea wouldn't get many event invites.

What Brandi wanted to avoid, if possible, was Chelsea's own

child seeing his mother interact with his teacher like that. The poor child seemed slow to open up to others, and that kind of negative experience could make it worse. She also didn't want the other children to think less of him simply because his mother was demanding. It was necessary, then, to speak to Chelsea privately in her office. She will have to insist that Chelsea come to talk to her and hope she doesn't throw a fit like one of the children.

The thought of Chelsea throwing a fit like a toddler in front of a bunch of children was entertaining, but assertiveness wasn't Brandi's specialty. She'd never had to be so assertive, and she needed to at least try and get through to Chelsea. She was sitting in her office, finishing up some billing and clerical issues, when there came a knock on the glass pane window of the door. Shea was standing there with a grimace, opening the door slowly.

"Chelsea just pulled into the lot," she said, glancing at the front door. "Got this?"

"Yes," Brandi said, standing stiffly. She strode from the office, Shea smirking at her as she disappeared back into the main classroom. Most of the children had already been picked up, and there were a couple still playing a game, including Chelsea's son, Grayson.

Brandi had been prepping herself, hyping herself up, trying to figure out what exactly she wanted to say. She contemplated her tone, words, and reactions, completely overthinking everything all afternoon. Of course, when Chelsea came walking through the door, eyes on her phone, Brandi forgot all of that.

"Good afternoon, Chelsea. Can we—?"

"Why weren't the children fed earlier like I requested?" Chelsea interrupted, glancing up from her phone. "I told you why Grayson needed to be fed earlier, right? So, why aren't they eating earlier?"

"If we could step into my office, I'll be happy to talk about—"

"No, I can say what I need right here," Chelsea scoffed, looking past Brandi toward Grayson and the other children still playing. Shea was close by, alerting the other assistants to Chelsea's prescience.

"That's not—"

"You're an educator, a childcare specialist, so when a parent tells you that their child needs something, you should listen," Chelsea continued, still looking at her phone. "If a parent told you their child couldn't have meat, you'd comply, yes?"

"Yes, but this is not—"

"And you have a nutritionist on staff? And you said the one girl was trained in CPR and first aid?" she asked, looking directly at Brandi now. "So maybe she can explain the information in the email I sent you. You did get the email?"

"Email?"

"You didn't even read the email?" she asked, rolling her eyes and looking back at her phone. "I know I sent it."

"I will have to check our company email and my personal one," Brandi affirmed, relieved to see Shea bringing Grayson out to the main lobby and cubby storage. He looked worried, his bright eyes wide as Shea helped him into his backpack and jacket.

"Please, do," Chelsea responded, her attitude worse as she turned to her son. "Ready?"

"Yes."

"I'm glad we had this talk," Chelsea said, turning from them, Grayson following as she left through the double doors. Even the way she walked was completely infuriating to Brandi, and she had to stop herself from swearing aloud as another parent came through the doors to pick up the last two children.

"An email," Brandi sighed when the friendly but busy mother of twins left, Shea locking the doors behind her.

"What about it?" she asked, glancing over her shoulder at Brandi.

"I could have just sent all of this in an email!" she groaned. Shea, Lehna, and Alyza were all frowning at her now, shaking their heads as she sat down at the front desk and logged onto the computer.

"That woman is a—"

"Don't say it," Brandi warned, shaking her head. "I swear, she's not human. Did you see how poor Grayson reacted when he had to leave?"

"You don't think something is going on at home, do you?" Lehna asked, eyes wide.

"That little boy is a sweetheart, but his mom is a piece of work," Alyza said, rolling her eyes. "I mean, really? Like we're supposed to change up everyone's schedule to accommodate *her* son? Lady... I don't think so."

"Right?" Lehna grumbled. "And she doesn't treat Brandi with any respect at all. Why didn't you speak up? Isn't that what you were working up to?"

"I was, but I should have put all of this in an email," Brandi said. "An email is neutral, professional, and a great medium to not have to interact with her in person. She can't interrupt an email!"

"Good point..." Shea shrugged, turning to the closet. "You type out your wordy email, and we'll clean up."

"Thank you," Brandi said, turning back to smile at them. "I should have thought about this earlier, and I feel so silly."

"No need, write your email," Lehna smirked, turning to help Shea.

Brandi couldn't believe she hadn't thought about writing an email to Chelsea. She could have confronted her, shut her down, and explained the policies more clearly in an email. Brandi didn't know how she could be so distracted and wondered about it before typing out her lengthy, four-paragraph email. She read, edited, reread, and then attached a copy of their school policies, which Chelsea signed when she enrolled Grayson.

When Alyza, Shea, and Lehna returned from their tidying and cleaning, she offered to let them read it. Shea and Lehna thought it was perfect, professional, and assertive. Alyza, however, didn't think she was being brutal enough. She also suggested that Brandi add some suggestions for homework and home care that would help him develop his speech. He was able to speak, but he wasn't initiating conversations or approaching the other children openly.

"No, that's more like criticism," Brandi explained, unwilling to go that far. "Let's just see how this goes first. Worst case scenario, she'll withdraw him from our care. There's nothing I can do about that, but I won't send it until tomorrow morning after she's dropped him off."

She was exhausted from that encounter, locking up behind the others and responding to her messages and chats from Nevaeh. It wasn't until Brandi was walking home that she remembered she had to go to the library again soon. The excitement that elicited was a bit different than it had been before. The anticipation of a new book mingled with the want to see Chris again was curious and addicting. Although, it caused her to feel conflicting emotions since one part of her wanted to explore the feelings, while the other part wanted to refrain since his future in Sweetgum was unclear. Being close to him was indescribable, despite her excessive knowledge of romance books.

Even her favorite author wouldn't be able to describe how she felt. Brandi was afraid of this feeling but equally fascinated, wanting to see where it led. She just hoped that it wouldn't lead to a dead end. She honestly couldn't imagine the library without Chris anymore, and that was where the fear set back in. Soon, she'd have to speak with Mrs. Everly and see what was wrong with her.

CHAPTER THIRTEEN

It was after six when he was able to lock the doors for the night and walk up the street to the grocery store. His hometown was so small; the local grocery store and bakery was the only one within walking distance of anywhere in town. It shared the parking lot of the convention center and dance studio, and it wasn't usually crowded.

Most people had to drive the fifteen minutes to their nearest Walmart and preferred it. Chris preferred the local shop, a friend of his grandmother owning it for his whole childhood until her son, a friendly guy with a small family, took it over just before Chris left for university. Today the parking lot was quite full, and there were some familiar friendly faces. Demetrius was coming out of the shop with his weekly hoard of snacks and drinks, usually for his weekly Magic and D&D matches at Nerd Central.

A couple of the older women his grandmother knew were in the parking lot, talking and laughing, waving kindly as he passed by. He smiled at them and nodded, eager to get inside and find something he might want for dinner. He found himself browsing the junk-food aisle for a few minutes, assaulted by all sorts of options, before turning toward the next set of aisles. He'd settle for a frozen pizza and a 6-pack but knew that probably wasn't the best option. Instead, he'd make something he always loved – turkey chili.

He had the ground turkey, a can of navy beans, peppers, and fresh tomato sauce in his basket when the smell of fresh bread and pastries caught his attention. He turned from the clear glass doors of the desert section immediately, striding around the corner toward the open and mostly empty bakery section. He wanted whatever smelled so good but was stopped in his tracks by a familiar form. Her curves were recognizable, even from behind. The way Brandi held a dainty little cake in her palm while she browsed cookies made his heart skip and his wide grin ache.

"Come here often?" Chris asked, striding up beside her with a smirk. He adjusted his glasses, tilting his head to observe the tiny pastry she held. She had jumped slightly, her intense brown eyes growing wide with shock.

"Oh," she breathed slightly. "I didn't see you there, and yes, I do come here quite often. Fresh pastries are always the best."

"How are you doing?" he asked, hoisting his library bag over his shoulder.

"To be honest, not that great," she sighed, a grimace on her now downcast face. Chris was a bit shocked at her response. His mind raced with all the possibilities of her discomfort and sadness, eager to know more. "That's probably why I'm buying some comfort food."

The smile that lit up her face again as she turned directly to him was blinding. The sparkle of kindness and optimism he had seen in her when they first met radiated. He didn't care if she was eating for comfort or not; he just cared that it made her happy again. He also cared that, however brief, she'd let that wall down that he was all too familiar with. He had that same wall and kept it up, the gate firmly locked at times. Perhaps that's why he was drawn to her, her openness and romantic optimism slapping him when he started reading off that list of books a couple of short weeks ago.

"Do you want some help eating that cake?" he questioned, her brown eyes wide again. He then held up the package of ground turkey from his small basket. "And maybe some dinner to go with it?"

"Feel free to say no," he blurted when she blushed, her smile growing as he babbled. "But I was going to make myself some turkey chili, so if you want, you can come to my place. At the very least, you could tell me about your terrible day and eat some comfort food. But feel free to say no; I'd just like to be there for you… if I can…."

Brandi smiled wider, her face like a beacon, hard to look at as he felt a rush of nervousness. He adjusted his glasses before glancing at the cookies on the table between them. He might have been a bit too forward and slightly stereotypical, but his experience with women wasn't what everyone might expect. He'd spent most of his time on academics, not dating.

"That sounds really good," she admitted, nodding happily. "I'd love to. I'll bring cake and cookies."

"I was going to get something to drink…."

"I've got juice and water." She nodded at her own small reusable bag. She then grabbed some chocolate chip cookies in a small paper container and put them in her bag. "What were you going to drink? I saw the soft drinks were on sale…."

"That sounds good," he said, turning with her back toward the beverage aisle.

She smiled, joked, and teased him about all the choices of soda, her dark silky hair falling from its bun and becoming looser by the moment. When they had paid and were back outside in the parking lot, the strong late winter breeze loosened her hair the rest of the way. It was now swaying and dancing around her shoulders and face as she tried to desperately re-pin it. Chris was happy to hold her bag while she pinned up her hair as tightly as she could. When she did, she laughed and took her bag back, offering for him to walk alongside her. It seemed they had both walked that day, Brandi zipping up her jacket as they strolled toward Main Street.

Neither of their houses was far from the main street, both living in the residential district between downtown and the school. It was a convenient walk to the library for work, and Chris didn't mind that his small duplex, a bachelor pad, caused him to street park. Unless he was leaving town, Chris preferred to walk everywhere. It seemed Brandi didn't mind either, the two of them talking about how much the town had changed since they were both in school. It fascinated Chris that he'd never known her before, being a few years older.

They walked past downtown onto the residential streets. They spoke nostalgically about friends who used to live in the old neighborhood before housing developments came in behind the school and hospital. They finally approached his home, Chris proud of the old southern early-century family home converted into two apartments. Its dark shutters, white frames, and forest green paint made it stand out amongst the surrounding white and grey buildings.

"My grandmother found this place for me when I moved back; it's a two-bedroom, two-bath," Chris explained, unlocking the door on the right, marked "2". "Her best friend's daughter is a local landlord, so I got lucky."

"It's beautiful; I remember it from when I was a child," she admitted, staring around the worn but large front porch that the two apartments shared. "It was a family home then, though I can't remember who lived here. My friend lived down the street...."

"Come in, I'll make us some dinner, and you can tell me all about your bad day," he insisted, allowing her through. The air was a bit stale, which he felt embarrassed by, so he quickly shut the door behind her and walked into the redesigned kitchen in the back. It was modernized but still old, with linoleum on the floor, and the countertops were a worn and dark granite. He cracked the living room window and kitchen window before unpacking his bag of groceries.

"Gladly," she replied, watching him from the living space in front. A small central room held the bathroom door and stairs between the kitchen and living space. It was a nice little area where he had put a small square card table and some mismatched wooden chairs.

"It's not exactly furnished how I would like, but it will do." He smiled wryly, opening his fridge. "My brother and dad brought the couch from their den, and my mom gave me every kitchen extra she had. She even had an extra set of chef knives! She can be a bit of a hoarder…."

"That's how my dad is with electrical components," she said, laughing. "But I think your place is cozy."

"Flatterer," he smirked, slipping out of his shoes, and shoving them in the nearest closet, then going over to the sink to wash his hands. "Let me get you a cup and some ice for your soda."

"No need; I usually drink from the bottle." She shrugged, setting her bag down with the cake and drinks on the counter beside him. "Can I help?"

"No, you sit down, have a drink, and tell me about your bad day," he insisted, grabbing the ingredients from various cabinets and containers. "I can cook and listen at the same time. I'm just that talented…."

"You're incorrigible," she said, grabbing her bottle of soda and sitting at his small table. "But I'll vent because I've run into a wall."

"Wall?"

"There's this new student, and he's fantastic, a bit shy, withdrawn, even a bit sad," Brandi explains, making sure not to specify who the student was. "But he isn't the problem – it's his mother."

"Uh-oh..." Chris said, turning on the stove and setting the pot atop it. It was one of the older ones his mom had given him, the wooden spoon propped over it as he started laying out a cutting board.

"She's challenging to deal with," Brandi said, opening her soda and watching him. "I mean, she comes in whenever she feels like it, leaves whenever she wants, doesn't give anyone a chance to speak, makes demands to change our schedule, and then she has the gall to criticize me for not meeting her demands. I mean, she's the one who signed our policies and all the intake paperwork when she signed her son up!"

"I might be a bit conflict-avoidant," Brandi admitted. Chris was still listening, chopping the veggies and throwing them in the pan with the simmering ground turkey. "But it's not like I've never had to stand up for myself. I'm not a total pushover; I've just never dealt with anyone so absolutely determined to bull-doze over me!"

"I decided that instead of confronting her, I'm just going to send a response to her rude email," Brandi shrugged before taking a sip from her soda bottle. "I'll lay out our expectations for parents at daycare, highlight the intake paperwork and policy she signed, and tell her in a very professional but strict manner that she can go... fly a kite."

"Nice recovery," he smirked, chuckling at her intentional avoidance of vulgarity. His grandmother disliked vulgarity and believed in using vocabulary to make your point, something Brandi clearly knew and mirrored.

"I haven't sent the email yet, but I will tomorrow," Brandi grumbled, pinching the bridge of her nose in frustration. "I mean, she can't argue or interrupt an email!"

"True," Chris said, putting the lid on the pot while the veggies and meat simmered together. "But I don't think this kind of conversation can be had strictly over email. Whoever this mom is, she sounds like the kind of person who thrives on conflict."

"You think so?" Brandi asked, sitting up straight. Her eyes had gone wide again, their brightness twinkling in the dim lights on his ceiling.

"Well, that's just my opinion." He smiled, putting some of the dirty dishes in the sink. "But you need to tell her that it's time for a serious sit-down and conversation. Getting into such a sensitive discussion via email wouldn't go very well. You can't read tone in the email, and this mom seems like she'll read too much into it emotionally, you know?"

"You're probably right," Brandi sighed, her eyes downcast. "It's just so difficult to talk to her face-to-face. She interrupts, walks away, or ignores me entirely."

"Well, what do you do when the children do that?" Chris questioned, stirring the meat and veggies before adding some stewed tomatoes and the beans. "I'd try dealing with her like you do with the children. Be direct, firm, but kind."

"I can give it a try." Brandi shrugged, smiling as he grabbed his drink from the fridge. He turned down the stove and sat next to her, the spicy sweetness of the chili filling the apartment with its scent. "How did you become so wise, magical spirit guide?"

"Hilarious," he joked, sipping from his water. "I had to get pretty good at difficult conversations during my academic work as a teaching assistant and my email exchanges with advisors. If there was any possibility for offense to be taken, it was better to look the other person in the eye while saying it. That, I think, is the foundation of my historical curiosity."

"Really?" she asked, Chris feeling a bit too proud to show off his academic research and journey.

The rest of the evening was quite magical. They enjoyed some chili, conversation about some basic regional history, and

Chris could remember laughing and smiling more than he had in a long while. He was enjoying a story about her friend Courtney and eating a cookie when she stopped, her eyes growing wide.

"It's snowing!" she said, almost jumping from her seat at the table as she saw the flakes fall outside his kitchen window. "I love snow...."

"Then let's go out," he said, encouraging her. "I've got a scarf somewhere in my closet."

Chris slipped on his shoes and reached for his jacket, snatching up the stray scarf for Brandi. He handed it to her as she buttoned up her jacket around her. The two were outside in the backyard, a large yard shared with his quiet and elderly neighbor, watching as white flakes came falling from the dark cloudy sky. It was a warm year for snow, and it seemed impossible, but here it was, falling all over his green yard. Today had been much colder, and perhaps there was a cold front; he hadn't been keeping up with the weather. It was even accumulating in the trees, twinkling in his evergreen like it stood in a Christmas market.

"It's beautiful." Brandi smiled, her face painfully bright. She was spinning in the snow, holding out her hands as it fell heavily. She might have seemed a bit childish or odd to anyone else, but to Chris, she was beautiful. The falling white snow around her landed on her jacket and dark hair, twinkling in the light from the house like diamonds.

It was breathtaking, but Chris wanted to have some fun, scooping up some fallen snow into a tiny, dripping snowball. While her back was turned, he tossed it, watching the slush ball pop and slide down her sleeve. She gasped, laughing, before grabbing up her own snowball. The two threw a few snowballs, laughing around the backyard as she hid behind some bushes, the tree, and the clothesline pole. When Chris went to toss a larger snowball at her, he slipped, the snowball flying from his hand to the ground as he fell.

He landed with a laugh, and Brandi offered him a hand, giggling when she slipped in the grassy slush of the snow against him. It was when she pushed herself up, hovering over him with a bright smile, that he realized just how perfect she looked. The snow was falling around them, and the stars were twinkling beyond the dim lights of the town. Her eyes were deep, sparkling like the glimmer of snow all around them. She was the most beautiful woman he'd ever seen, and that moment felt absolutely perfect and a bit corny.

"I… I'm going to kiss you now," he breathed, their faces close. Her bright eyes grew wide, but she nodded, chewing her bottom lip.

The kiss was warm, passionate, and soft, something he'd never known he needed until she was here, in his arms. He held her close, gently caressing her jawline and neck with his fingertips as they kissed. Her lips parted when he licked her bottom lip, allowing him to taste her. It was sweet, spicy from the chili, and absolutely addicting. He could stay like this forever, holding her in his arms, but the fogging of his glasses and the chuckle on her lips pulled him back to reality.

CHAPTER FOURTEEN

Brandi felt like she was in one of her romance novels, her body reacting as Chris' lips consumed her. She'd never been kissed like this, feeling his soft tongue tease and explore her own lips and mouth. It was a heady, breathless feeling as he caressed her neck and cheek. She knew he was eager, his arm holding her gently as her hands grasped at the front of his jacket. She wanted to touch him, to be closer, pushing open the top of his jacket and running her cool palms up his neck to his jaw.

His hands gripped her hips now, holding her gently as the kiss deepened. This perfect moment of absolute bliss was unlike anything Brandi had ever hoped to experience. She loved it and felt a real loss when she had to pull away, a grin spreading over her blushing face. He seemed disoriented as well, breathing heavily as the two still held one another.

"Wow," she breathed, willing to admit it was intense and a bit steamy. "That was nice."

"Yeah?" he asked, looking a bit bashful. "Wasn't too much?"

"It was great," she whispered, adjusting his glasses for him.

"But it's cold and wet out here. So we should probably go back inside."

"R-right!" he said, standing from under her slowly as they both regained their feet. The ground was wet and peppered with snow. Chris allowed her to pass him and enter the apartment first.

Brandi felt excited, a bit nervous, and unsure if she should suggest they continue. Truthfully, she wanted to continue, to be like those angsty characters in her novels, but she decided against it. So instead, she wiped her shoes on the mat carefully before slipping them off. She held them as she sat back down at the table, forgetting that the cake and cookies were even there. Chris followed, shoving his shoes and jacket into the closet before offering to take the scarf back from Brandi.

"S-sorry." She smiled, offering it to him. "I s-should probably get going anyway."

"Oh?" he asked, the surprise behind his response encouraging.

"It was really a great evening," she explained, rambling again. "That chili was delicious, and I can't believe it snowed. You can keep the cookies if you like…."

"I'd love to do it again sometime," Chris admits as she puts the plastic top on the tiny cake. "If… you want."

"I really would," she agreed. A bright smile had come over his face, adjusting his steamed glasses. His bright brown eyes intense as he removed the thick rectangular lenses and considered her.

"How about this Sunday?" he asked, knowing that was the only day he would have off from the library.

"That sounds great!" she said, pulling her phone out. "Let's exchange numbers."

"Right!" he said, seeming to forget about his phone entirely. He pulled it from the kitchen counter, sharing his number and social media. Brandi was ecstatic to have his contact information, becoming flustered when she realized what day Sunday was. Chris noticed her nervous chuckle and glanced at her phone curiously.

"Sunday." Brandi smiled, admiring how sexy he was, with or without his glasses. "It's the 14th."

"14th?" he asked, looking lost.

"It's… Valentine's day…."

O-oh," he chuckled, rubbing the back of his neck, his lean but toned muscles flexing above her. "I didn't realize. We can reschedule if you'd like."

"Do you want to?" she asked, feeling too optimistic about her Valentine's plans.

"Do *you*?" he asked. "I mean, I want to see you again, no matter what day, but if you think it's weird that our first date is on Valentine's Day, then we can change it."

"There's no need to change it," she admitted, stepping closer. "Let's meet then."

"Sounds good; I'll plan something nice," he said, his smile soft. "It will be a surprise…."

"A surprise?" She smirked, appreciating his creativity and enthusiasm.

"A surprise," he whispered, stepping closer.

He was taller than her, thin but agile, and she wanted to melt into those bright brown orbs of his. They were intoxicating, the flecks of brown and umber enchanting her as his lips gently hovered over hers. They brushed when he spoke, his scent just as intoxicating as the heat of his body.

"I'll show you more of who I am, though I'm a bit odd if you haven't noticed." He smiled, gently pecking her lips, lingering there as he laced his fingers with hers. "I wear many masks, as my grandmother would say."

"Love takes off the masks that we fear we cannot live without and know we cannot live within," Brandi quoted, thinking of the famous line by James Baldwin.

"That's right," Chris breathed, his eyes growing wide and his smile brightening everything about the room as he wrapped an arm around her.

The crushing, beautifully intense, yearning kiss they shared there, lingering in his living room, was hypnotic. She didn't want to stop, Brandi's hand wrapping around his neck as he held her sensually close to his body. It was an earth-shattering kiss that she eventually pulled away from with shaky breath and quivering lips.

"I-I'll see you Sunday," she breathed, capturing his lips again before turning with her bag to leave. He offered to give her a ride, but she wanted to walk the short distance. She glanced over her shoulder at his house when she turned down the sidewalk, having to go just three blocks over to her own street. She felt the fire inside her, the flurry of butterflies strong as she walked in the cool night air. It was still lightly snowing as she turned down her road, and she could still smell his scent on her jacket.

She had to get a grip to understand that this was the real world and not some cheesy romance novel. She loved romance, she loved love, but she couldn't possibly fall for a man who might not stick around Sweetgum. She didn't want to leave here, growing up here and hoping to one day have a life and family in the community. She wasn't opposed to adventure, to travel, but she wanted this to be the home her children knew. How could she have that when she wasn't even sure if Chris was going to stay long?

"I'm not sure my heart could take it," she sighed, unlocking her door and entering the small home with the nice fence and yard.

CHAPTER FIFTEEN

Chris was lying on his bed, staring haplessly at the ceiling on this gray, cool, late-winter morning. His mind was overrun, and he couldn't put it into words; the sensation was a mixture of all his emotions. It was as if he'd kept his emotional tap firmly fastened, and suddenly, without warning, the tap was released. Flooding his mind like a broken dam, all Chris could think about was Brandi. What she was doing, what she would think of his thoughts, what flirty thing he'd say next, and about a million other scenarios and instances that he just couldn't keep up with.

He'd never felt like this before, an undeniable confusion permeating these sappy thoughts of infatuation, intimacy, and shared experiences. He wasn't that kind of guy, wasn't that romantic, and to find himself confronted with such a stereotypical romantic reaction was equally infuriating and intoxicating. What was he going to do? Was he really falling for Brandi, or was he just desperate to have someone, like most people were? Was there more to it?

He hadn't even gotten out of bed yet, waking before his alarm at seven. He had lain there for a long while before finally picking up his charged phone. He was surprised to see a text message had come in ten minutes ago, the phone still on silent notification. He was equally surprised to see it was Nate. Wondering why his friend was texting him so early, Chris read the message, replying promptly.

NATE:

Hey! It's early, but what's up? How is it going with the library girl? I've got meetings all day...

CHRIS:

Her name is Brandi, and it's complicated. Meetings?

Complicated? What's complicated? She's your type. And just some local stuff.

That's the problem. I think I'm really falling for her.

That's not a problem. That's a solution. Are you still applying to jobs out of state?

Yeah, but I'm not holding my breath. They are very competitive.

And you are great at your job. Passion! So, I wouldn't count yourself out.

The chance of me being chosen for an interview is slight, so I'm not worried.

Maybe you should think about that possibility anyway. Just in case...

Yeah... you're probably right...

Chris put his phone down now, forcing himself out of bed and into the bathroom for his regular morning routine. He decided that a simple pair of slacks, a collared button-up, and a thin but plain gray sweater vest would be comfortable that morning. He decided to walk the couple of blocks to the library, rolling up the sleeves of his shirt to his elbows. Grabbing a light windbreaker and slipping into his comfortable but practical slip-on office shoes, he was about to leave when his phone rang. He was surprised by the face and name on the phone screen, answering immediately.

"Hello," he said, smiling as he stood just outside his front door. He was locking it, ready to walk to work as he spoke to his elusive grandmother. "How are you feeling this morning, granny?"

"Don't granny me," she said, her voice warbling. "What's this, I hear? You want to try out some community events at the library?"

"Well, we already have a reading circle for the little ones, but one for the older children, yes. We also have some suggestions from the community about events they'd like to see," Chris explained, knowing his grandmother would need persuading. He descended his front porch and stoop, strolling happily down the empty sidewalk toward the library.

"A suggestion box?" she replied, her voice sharp, somewhat irritated. "Chris… are you sure you want to take this on? I mean, doing community events is great, but you have to be consistent."

"I'm consistent, granny," he smirked, stopping at an intersection before crossing. "Besides, I can at least start a community involvement program and see how it goes, can't I? If it doesn't work, no one will mind…."

"Well, if you're sure you're committed," she sighed, her voice becoming soft. "How's it going, by the way? Enjoying yourself?"

"More than I thought," he admitted, waving kindly at a neighbor walking their terrier. "It's been a real learning experience for me, in more ways than one."

"Good, I'm glad to hear that," she insisted, her voice lowering. "Tell me; your mother says you met a girl…."

"This is not the time, granny," Chris quirked his lips,

knowing how much of a gossip and a schemer she was. "I'll talk to you about it when I come to visit next, okay?"

"When will that be?" she asked, her voice hitching.

"I'll call," he explained, walking down the block toward the next street, where the library sat. "Get well soon, all right? There are people here who miss you...."

"Ah, my lovely girl Brandi," his grandma sighed, sounding wistful. "I miss her very much. Tell her that for me, will you?"

"The next time I see her." He smiled, turning the corner and crossing another street. The library was just ahead, the old brick and stone façade capped with a small clock tower and wind vane. "Get some rest; I'll call you again tonight."

"You're a good boy," she sighed, her voice soft. "Have a good day, Chris."

"You too, granny." He smiled, hearing the click on the other end.

The moment he opened that library door, using the side entrance around back in the parking lot, he felt emotionally drained. Everything in there reminded him of his grandma or Brandi, and his heart fluttered. He needed to focus on the task at hand to be the best librarian he could be for their small community. He needed to refocus his efforts on his passion for history and literature. So after opening the front doors at nine, he got right to the suggestion box, reading through all of them quickly. The thought of painful truths sinking into his core was slow but reflective as he applied hard truths to his situation.

Chris needed to understand the truth of himself, his truth, and his feelings for this girl that had come into his life like the crack of lightning. He'd been so perfectly content, happy to be back home, and now his joy was multiplied infinitely. But, ever since he'd met Brandi, ever since they'd started to expand on their relationship, something had felt different, amplified. It was like those whimsical moments in epic fantasy, where the protagonist is suddenly shifted, altered, because of the prescience of someone they love. It was heady, intoxicating, and dangerous beyond reason, which was what frightened and enthralled Chris.

He shook himself from his thoughts, ready to tackle the big issue of the day. Rummaging through the suggestions was one thing, but now he just had to decide which events to start with. Going through the papers the teens filled out, Chris realized Brandi was right to have him take teen input. Not even one suggested tabletop games, but several had suggested a craft club. Other suggestions included a movie night, a photography club, and an art club.

Chris decided to go easy, starting out with a craft club. He picked up the phone at the desk, the patrons mostly drawn into their books or the computers. He stood in the office doorway, grabbing the phone number of the mother who reached out to him when he first got here. The phone rang three times before a young voice answered on the other end.

"Hello?"

"Uh… hello. I'm looking for Caroline," Chris replied, unsure how to talk to the child on the other end. "I'm the librarian here at Sweetgum Library. Is Caroline home?"

"Yeah, one minute," the child replied, a loud holler in the background making Chris grimace. "Momma! Momma! Phone!"

"Ty! What did I tell you about answering my phone?!"

"It's a violation of privacy and bad manners," the boy replied begrudgingly.

"Go, get your shoes on! We're already late for school!" There was a shuffling on the line, and then a polite but exasperated voice rang out. "Hello? So sorry about that…."

"Not a problem, this is Chris with Sweetgum Library," Chris explained. "I was hoping you might have some time to discuss your thoughts for community day events."

"Oh! You got some feedback from the suggestion box?" she

asked excitedly. "I've got time after I drop the children off at school. Would you like me to stop in?"

"That'd be most kind," he admitted, smiling into the phone. "I thought about what you said and took some input from some teens, and I think a craft club is a great place to start."

"Wonderful! I agree and would love to stop in this morning, say, twenty minutes?"

"Sounds great. I'd love your input, and I hope you'd be open to chaperoning," he explained, his smile growing wider as he realized she was genuinely excited. "See you soon, Caroline."

CHAPTER SIXTEEN

*B*randi was nervous that Sunday morning, excited about their first date this evening, but a bit embarrassed by the fact that it was on Valentine's Day. Embarrassed might not have been the word, as she would have gone anywhere with Chris at any time. She was self-conscious about the date simply because the pressure between falling for him completely and striving to keep it shallow was back and forth. It wasn't as if she could plunge headlong into this romance without restraint – there was significant hesitation and fear in her whenever she thought about it.

As she checked her reflection one more time, she couldn't help but admire the outfit she and her girlfriends had picked out. It was a classic winter outfit, long black leggings, a mid-length warm woolen sweater dress, a cozy half-jacket, and a scarf. She'd decided not to flat iron her hair today, and around her head, holding her naturally curly and wavy dark hair out of her eyes, was a simple black headband. She loved the cute boots as well; they were practical and warm. She was excited to see what Chris had planned for their date. She was to meet him downtown, where winter-themed Valentine's festivities were going on.

As she parked her car at the daycare center, she noticed Chris was already there, waving at her happily as she stepped out to greet him. He was dressed quite smartly. He wore a slate peacoat, a casual pair of denim jeans, a pair of Timberlands, and an adorably colorful scarf around his neck. She embraced him when they met, smiling shyly when he wrapped his arms around her as well.

"How was the rest of your week?" he asked, offering her his arm as they pulled apart slowly.

"I didn't send the email," she sighed. "But we can talk about all that another time. I'm curious about our date… what would you like to do?"

"Well, I was thinking we could try some ice skating," he said, pointing toward the small indoor rink at the nearby park. "And perhaps we could keep it casual, fun? Go to Roasted Beans after for a coffee and chat?"

"That sounds wonderful," she admitted, squeezing his arm tightly. "I'm quite good at ice skating, you know."

"I've never tried," Chris admits. "But you're a great teacher, I've heard, so we can do this."

"I see." She smiled, leaning against his arm as they walked across the street toward the rink and the few people who were there that particular Sunday evening.

After renting the skates, a tutorial on putting them on from Brandi, and a wobbly trudge to the rink, they were both finally ready. Chris felt a bit foolish; the only people there were a few children and random couples. However, Brandi's encouragement and the way she held his arm, helping him stay upright as they slowly started gliding, was warming. Chris's face flushed, and he felt a bit tired from falling and trying to maintain his balance, but Brandi didn't mind.

They laughed, chatted about how she'd learned, and Chris even admitted he was having a lot of fun, despite being so bad. Brandi had been able to glide right across the rink with him, smiling the whole way as he became more confident and balanced. It had been barely an hour when Chris was finally able to slowly but smoothly glide around the edges of the rink without holding onto her.

"I've got this." He smiled, Brandi skating up effortlessly to glide next to him.

"You're doing great!" Brandi smiled, holding out her cold ungloved hand. When Chris took it happily, his eyes widened, realizing she was cold for the first time. He pulled her closer, slowly stopping as she brought her fingers up to his face.

"So cold," he whispered, clasping them between his cupped hands and warming them with his breath. "You want to go to Roasted Beans now? Get something warm to drink and eat?"

"I don't know." She smiled, pressing closer to him. "I kind of like where we are right now."

She was elated to see the nervous smile on his face, a grimace forming before he kissed her lips gently, sweetly. She enjoyed the short but gentle kiss, trembling when he pulled her close to him, intentionally leaning against the wall of the rink. Finally, he pulled away, gently tightening her scarf around her neck before kissing her forehead.

"Let's go get something warm to drink and discuss further," he whispered, his breath hot on her ear.

After removing their skates, slipping back into their warm boots, and walking around the corner to the coffee shop, Brandi stopped him before they went in. It was a quiet Sunday night for the shop; Brandi realized Joanne wasn't working that night, just a couple of her college-aged baristas. Nevertheless, she didn't want to go in just yet, unwilling to share Chris with anyone else in the café, including the onlookers or locals who were sometimes inconveniently friendly.

"What's wrong?" he asked, eyes wide and glowing in the light of the café windows. "Are you feeling all right?"

"Just… happy," she sighed, surprised by her response. She was beyond happy, making his genuinely charming smile even brighter. "I just… wanted to say that."

"I'm happy, too," he replied, turning fully toward her. He leaned down, pressing his forehead to hers with a grimace. "But I know you're cold; even your lips are turning blue."

She smiled but gasped happily when his lips found hers again, intoxicatingly warm and slow. It was a passionate kiss, something she melted into enthusiastically. She clutched the collar of his jacket, pulling him closer as they stood in the shadow of the awning, making out. Brandi didn't care if anyone saw Chris' hands gently roaming her curves before they came up for air.

"Let's go in before we end up devouring one another instead," Chris said, a puff of steam coming from their mingled breaths as they laughed.

Inside, after removing their jackets and sitting comfortably on a couch in the dimmed corner, a kind barista who Brandi recognized took their orders. They each got a homemade stuffed pastry, some cocoa, and a shared piece of coffee cake, the barista happy to facilitate their privacy. When she disappeared, Chris turned to Brandi, smiling as she nestled under his arm.

"So, the tough parent," Chris smirked, making her brow furrow.

"I didn't send the email, but I still don't know how to confront her," Brandi sighed, staring at the coffee table in front of them. "I just don't know if I can do it."

"Well, maybe we can approach it from a different angle," Chris offered, pushing some of her hair back from her headband. It had gotten loose during their skating, and he enjoyed the little whisps and curls falling into her face. "Don't think of it as a confrontation but a conversation, a lesson to be learned.

"I mean, it's like teaching a child in some ways." Chris shrugged, keeping his arm around her shoulders. "She's got to respect your authority as the teacher, and I know you have it in you to teach all sorts of students."

"I do, and it really isn't fair to the other students, parents, or her own child," Brandi sighed, thinking of her son's downcast face whenever his mom spoke to Brandi. "Her own child knows she's in the wrong. I can see the shame in his face…."

"Poor child…"

"He deserves a good school experience!" Brandi groaned, becoming a bit too passionate about her feelings. "And she needs to understand that I'm in charge of my own daycare."

"Get 'em," he smirked, kissing her forehead as the barista came back with a tray of cocoa, food, and silverware.

"Anything else?" she asked politely, admiring both Brandi and Chris.

"No, thank you." Brandi smiled happily, waving after her as she turned away. She then turned to Chris, picking up her cup of cocoa. "So, how goes the job searches? Applied to any good places?"

She didn't intend to mention it at all, meaning to keep it buried until he chose to tell her, but it surfaced quite abruptly, making them both grimace awkwardly. Brandi couldn't believe she'd ruined a perfect moment like that, but Chris didn't seem to mind. He just took a sip, set his cup down, and pulled her closer, his arm lowering around her waist as they spoke intimately.

"I've applied for a few jobs, one in Atlanta, two in D.C., one in Boston, and one in Detroit, but they're very competitive," Chris explained, his voice low and serious as he watched her face closely. She felt scrutinized but stared back, unwilling to back down. She hoped he could see the sadness in her eyes, the yearning for him to stay, but she didn't dare voice her hopes.

"You've got this," she said, touching his cheek gently. "You're brilliant; any museum or library would be lucky to have you."

"I needed that," he admitted, chuckling softly. "I'm such a perfectionist when it comes to work."

"Uhm, I hope you don't mind, but I can't seem to stop myself," Brandi admitted. She was staring at her lap and the cup of cocoa there, unsure how to ask this. "But do you want to leave Sweetgum?"

The pause was unbearable, several breaths passing between them until Chris frowned, his voice wavering but resolute. It was heartbreaking, brave, and beautiful, and Brandi could only focus on that, wanting desperately to change the subject afterward.

"Well, I'm not sure what I'd do with my degree here, in such a small town," Chris said, still holding her close around her waist. His other hand crept forward, gently touching her fingertips as she held the cup of cocoa.

"Whatever you decide, you mustn't stay away forever," Brandi said, smiling brightly up at him, which took all her energy.

She needed to change subjects, to stop thinking about Sweetgum without Chris. It was a sinking, lingering, horrible feeling, and it needed to be gone. It was their first date, and she didn't need it marred by sadness and her own bad judgment.

"Of course not." Chris smiled, holding her close. The warmth of his body, the hum of electricity between them, was as painful as it was pleasurable.

Brandi and Chris whispered, discussing their favorite books and movies, and then Brandi learned more about Chris's interest in tabletop games. She was also surprised and excited that he and Demetrius were friends. Demetrius was the grumpy but lovable comic-shop owner, and she loved seeing him at the library and around town. She had no idea Chris was into all of this and wondered how she could learn more about Dungeons and Dragons. A quick Google search earlier this week didn't help and succeeded in confusing her with various manuals and versions.

An hour later, during some lingering kisses and soft laughter, Brandi realized the coffee shop would be closing soon. She pulled away from Chris, her hand lingering in his as she stood. He was confused for a second and then noticed the baristas putting chairs up and cleaning behind the counter.

"Thanks, ladies." Chris smiled and waved, leaving them a fifty-dollar bill on the table. "Keep the change for a tip!"

"Thanks, guys! Come again!" the waitress called, waving as the two buttoned up their jackets and slipped out the door into the cold.

Chris happily walked Brandi back to her car, their arms wrapped around one another warmly. When they got across the street and down the block to the parking lot, he paused, leaving her at her car.

"Can you wait here just one second?" he asked, smiling slyly.

"Okay..."

Brandi watched as he went to his own car, went inside, and returned with something in his hand. It wasn't until he was a few feet away that she realized what he held. He was coming back with a heart-shaped box of chocolates and a bouquet of flowers.

"No! You didn't have to get me these! We just started seeing each other," she giggled, loving the Valentine's gifts.

"I wanted to get them for you," he admitted, blushing brightly in the light of the parking lot lamps. "I mean, it might be too corny, and that's why I left them in my car. But... it's Valentine's Day, and even though this is a first date, you deserve flowers and chocolate on Valentine's Day."

"Thank you." She smiled, holding them in her hands gently.

When she looked back up into his brown eyes, she felt something inside her explode. She had a desperate need to hold him, to feel him in her arms, and she reacted. Without thought, without reservation, she wrapped her arms around his shoulders and captured his lips hungrily.

It was so passionate and so warm. They had been standing there kissing, holding one another, for a long while in reality, both shivering from the cold of the night. However, Brandi could have stood there all night as long as she was in his arms. He must have felt the same way, recapturing her lips every time she pulled away. However, soon they were both shivering, out of breath, and ready to depart. Chris watched her leave the parking lot, waving slowly as she pulled away, that warm feeling inside her still there when she finally calmed down enough to get into bed that night.

CHAPTER SEVENTEEN

"How's it going today?" Brandi asked, leaning across the library desk. "Been busy?"

"Caroline popped in this morning," Chris said, having gotten to know the craft mom better. She was so helpful in starting up the children's craft club, but what Chris really wanted help with was the teen craft club. He wasn't sure where to start and knew Brandi would have ideas. He was less reluctant to admit that he really wanted to see her again after their first date earlier that week. "So, good news all around, it would seem."

"Well, tell me then," she chuckled, sitting behind the desk with him to catalog the recent returns. "I'm all suspense."

"I thought you were all romance," Chris winked, making her blush. She then nudged him, rolling her eyes playfully.

"What's the good news?" she urged, smiling and waving at a familiar parent and their child coming in after school and sports practice.

"I've got the green light from granny," he smirked, waving at them as they passed. "She's allowed me the children's craft club, the teen craft club, and…."

"And..?!"

"A read-aloud story hour for the kiddies and board game night for teens and adults," Chris winked, putting away the recent donations that needed cleaning, coding, and cataloging. He was stacking them on the shelf in the office when he felt her familiar hand on his arm.

"That's a big deal," Brandi insisted, offering him a kind smile and a gentle hug. "Congratulations, the community is going to be so happy. We'll have to put it into the newsletter that goes out Friday."

"You're right!" Chris exclaimed, realizing he hadn't even made final edits to it or printed them. "I almost forgot about the newsletter."

"Don't panic." Brandi smiled, touching his face. "Deep breath, you've got this."

"I've got this," Chris said, thankful for her confidence. "So, would you like to help me finalize the newsletter and print them? I've still got to drop them at the post office tomorrow, but we could order dinner from Rochelle's and make an evening of it."

"Well, we close the library in 90 minutes?" she asked, glancing at the clock. "So yeah, let me text Rochelle, ask her about the specials, and then, while you edit, I'll shelve and catalog."

"You're too good," he smirked, kissing her cheek gently. "I've missed you."

"Yeah?" she questioned, whispering in his ear. "I've missed you, too."

"I hoped you would," he admitted, his hand touching the small of her back as they melded closer together in the small, secluded office. "How was your day?"

"The usual," she admitted, remembering Chelsea's little outburst when she once again came late for pickup. Chris noticed the change in her demeanor; his eyebrow raised curiously. "It's the difficult parent again… she had a fit when she picked her child up and is insisting on volunteering twice a week in the classroom. It's hard to tell her no."

"I thought you were going to talk to her?" Chris asked, concerned. "It's your classroom, your business essentially! She can't come in and tell you how to do your job, something you've been trained to do. That's just...."

"I know, I know," Brandi sighed, silencing him with a soft kiss. "I'm working on it, but it's hard for me...."

"I understand, and I don't want to push you, but at the same time," he whispered, her breath hot on his collar as he leaned closer. "You're a goddess in that daycare, and you should reign with authority."

"You're so enticing when you talk like that," Brandi smirked, her bright brown eyes twinkling up at him. "But we're in the office, at the library, and there are customers...."

"You're right," he conceded, his hand lingering on her hip before he turned back to the front desk outside.

The rest of the night before they closed was smooth, with Chris finishing the edits to the newsletter. He was happy to let Brandi read it but was reluctant to make the edits she suggested, the wording to her sounding a bit too formal to entice the children and teens. He altered a few phrases, and she rewarded him with one of her kind smiles that melted his heart.

"And now we print." Chris smiled, waving goodbye to the last of the patrons before locking the front doors behind them. He shut off the lobby and front lights a few minutes later, locking the back door and ensuring the library was indeed empty.

"They look great." Brandi smiled, admiring the newsletters as they printed. "Just a tri-fold?"

"Exactly, and I even pre-purchased the postage online so I can just drop them at the post office," he said, proud of his quick thinking.

"Just make sure you warn the clerk," Brandi chided, folding

the pamphlets carefully. "I'm sure the actual post office will give you a better rate, and it helps out the local employees at the post office."

"You think?" Chris asked, unsure why she was so picky about this. "I mean, there's what? Three employees?"

"Would you rather drive to the next town for your mail?"

"Fair point," he admitted, unwilling to argue with her over something so trivial. "I'll talk to the clerk tomorrow before I open."

"Thank you." She smiled, squeezing his arm. It was then that her phone rang, Rochelle's voice laughing over the other end. "Ah, yes, we're here. Come to the side door, Rochelle."

"I'll go unlock it," Chris offered, jumping up from the table they'd taken over with the six hundred or so pamphlets.

Rochelle was kind, bringing them extra dessert, hot cocoa, and two loaded boxes of food. Chris thanked her multiple times, not realizing how hungry he was. Rochelle just smiled, leaving them to their dinner in the library with a smirk and a wink at Brandi. Chris snickered at this, waving after her and locking the door again when she disappeared.

"She's such a character," he admitted, sitting back down at another table with Brandi, so they didn't ruin any of the papers. "Cocoa?"

"Yes, do you want the carrot cake or the red velvet?"

"Oh, carrot, please...."

The two enjoyed their meal, laughing, chatting, and losing track of time until the clock on the wall chimed eight, something Chris wasn't ready for. They hadn't even gotten through half of the pamphlets and knew it was going to take a while longer. It wasn't until after nine that they were done, the papers bound together by rubber bands and stacked neatly in a cardboard box.

"That was a lot." Brandi smiled, reading an extra one that

had gotten ripped. "But well worth it for all the community activities we've added for the next few weeks."

"Granny wasn't keen, but I'm glad she consented," he said, stretching and wrapping an arm around Brandi. "I'm excited to show you my collection of board games and everything."

"Yes, you are a big fan of board games," she said, gently wrapping her arms around him. "What kind of board games do you have?"

"All sorts, really," he said, steering her to one of the armchairs. The both of them sank into it, Brandi sitting almost on his lap as he held her close. It was intimate, the two of them perfectly content to chat and just be in one another's presence a while longer.

"Tell me," she sighed, sinking into his warmth.

"Well, I like classic board games like Monopoly or Life or Clue or something," he said, playing with some of her curly dark hair. "But I also like more complicated games like Ticket To Ride, Settlers of Catan, Warhammer, and my favorite will probably always be Dungeons and Dragons."

"Ah, I know Dungeons and Dragons," she said, having heard of it from Demetrius over and over again. "It's a dice and board game, right?"

"Yeah, except you keep track of your character with paper, like in Clue," he surmised, kissing her forehead. "It's a really fun game. I'd love to teach you sometime if you're willing."

"Demetrius has been trying to get me to play for a while, but I keep telling him I'm just clueless," Brandi chuckled, pecking him gently on the lips. "Maybe I need a teacher…."

"Happily," he cooed, a soft growl escaping his lips when she nibbled at him.

"We should close up and head home," Brandi offered, unwilling to move first.

"Would… w-would you like to sleep over?" Chris asked, both of them pausing nervously.

"Like...?"

"I don't mean sleep together, I promise," he corrected, his voice hitching slightly. "I-I just meant we can fall asleep together, cuddle, or maybe keep talking?"

"I'd like that, but I'd have to grab some things from home first," she said, blushing when he beamed down at her.

"I'll walk you if you want."

"Oh, I drove, but you can come with me, and we can walk back to your place," she said, glancing at her phone. "It's almost ten, so we better get going."

THE WEEK KEPT GOING like that, into the next week and their first craft night, which was a roaring success. The children loved it, and the teens enjoyed starting their crafts. Some were knitting, others were drawing, and some were sculpting with clay, which Chris could appreciate. Each child and teenager at those club meetings was excited and uniquely creative with everything they did. They even have some cultural art styles that were given to them inadvertently through their own family's local customs.

Chris was fascinated, enjoying the excitement and the noise in the usually quiet library that evening. Brandi, who had stopped in before closing to walk home with him, was just as excited as he was, praising all her former and current students as they all showed off their creations. Even the parents were thrilled, some volunteering to chaperone in the future.

Of course, some of the older children were even talking about game night, and Chris explained to them how they could make their own original characters, explore worlds created by Demetrius, and work together with a team to win fame and treasure. So many were interested, which excited him for their upcoming first game night. He didn't want to start with anything too complicated, but he knew he eventually wanted to incorporate D&D campaigns into board game night.

After closing the library and encouraging the children to think about their own characters, Chris and Brandi happily walked back to her house. They strode arm-in-arm, smiling, chatting, and laughing the whole way. Brandi had prepared him a special dinner, some homemade tatter-tot casserole with cheese and veggies.

The two enjoyed some cocoa, their dinners, and their new favorite streaming series about some royal drama from hundreds of years ago. It was somewhat fantastical, and that's probably why Chris found it amusing. However, Brandi absolutely adored the romantic moments, something Chris could appreciate about her. She was so utterly romantic and honest about it that it almost frightened him.

He wasn't sure how to be that honest about his emotions, especially about love, and knew that he had to get over that. He had to trust that there was love and that he could find a way forward with Brandi. After all, he hadn't really made up his mind about finding another job, and right now, he just wanted to enjoy being with her. She was like the sun to his moon, bright and glowing and completely overpowering.

She was also much more, his mind wandering to great literary romances and how the authors must have known how he was feeling in that moment at some point in their own lives. It was heartwarming, and as Brandi fell asleep, cheek to his chest, he watched her face. It was beautiful, shadowed in genuine happiness, something so rare it was painful to see. She had let it all out, allowing herself to commit to whatever their relationship was, and he admired her for it.

He was absolutely drawn into her, and it seemed to be unending devotion, like a waking dream that he feared would reach its end as all things did. He held her closer now, his grip tightening slightly as she sighed against him. He couldn't stand the idea of losing her in some romantically tragic and epic way. He couldn't imagine parting from her even for a short time, including going back out to California. That thought frightened him a bit, as he hadn't considered what he'd do beyond his grandmother's supposed sickness.

He hadn't decided to apply for any additional jobs or move along because knowing Brandi had put off all other thoughts of concerns. How could it not? She was exquisite, absolutely perfect for him in almost every single way. He just hoped she'd become more confident in herself and her inherent power. A lot of good could be done with that if she tried.

CHAPTER EIGHTEEN

"And so, the giant followed Jack as he climbed as quickly as he could down the beanstalk," Brandi read, flipping some picture pages for the little ones in the library. They were surrounding her, almost a dozen of them, each waiting to hear what happened next. Chris observed with an equal amount of fascination and wonder.

She was such a natural, and he loved her commitment to the bit, making different voices for almost every character. It was as if she was born to play D&D, and Chris admitted that he was very excited to introduce her to the game tonight. She, Demetrius, himself, Brandi's friend Neveah, two teens from the craft club, and two teens from the comic shop were all going to gather that night in the library for the first-ever Sweetgum Board Game Night.

"Of course, I've been doing small matches for close friends at my shop for years," Demetrius explained, smiling around the table. "So never fear, I've got all the dice, pencils, miniatures, and player sheets we could need. We're playing 5e, yes?"

"Whoah, whoah," Neveah stopped him, holding up her hand. "Slow down and explain from the beginning."

"All right, it's really simple once you understand." Chris chuckled, sitting next to Demetrius, who took the head of the table as the Dungeon Master. "We all get a character sheet, a set of dice, and a pencil."

"I also have a set of miniatures you may all choose from." Demetrius smiled, pulling out a small pencil case full of small, painted humanoid creatures.

"Right, so… since we've got some first-timers here, we'll take the first twenty minutes, or so, explaining how to set up your character," Chris explained, the teens from the comic shop already filling out their character sheets. "And 5e is the version of D&D we are playing; basically, a more streamlined version of the character sheet and other specifics that aren't really relevant right now."

"All right, so I can pick a character then?" one of the teen girls from the craft club asked, staring at her sheet. "How do I do that?"

Chris beamed as he explained all the character creation details, including looking at the Player's Manual for 5e and selecting preferred character archetypes. He was happy to see they had a balanced group to start out with, willing to take the role of melee damage as a human barbarian. The group had decided on their roles, their races, and classes, and rolled their stats within the first twenty minutes, and were debating which miniatures to use when a surprise visitor showed up.

It was Mrs. Zhang, eagerly handing out boxes of food from her restaurant to the hungry players. Chris appreciated the gesture, thanking Mrs. Zhang and the parents who put it together with Brandi and Demetrius, but what he really wanted to do was get to the game. He wanted to show Brandi how fun it was to play this game, insisting Mrs. Zhang might want to stay and learn. She declined, happy to deliver the food, and disappear again.

So, after they quickly ate, Chris started laying out the basic concepts of the game. He explained the squares as measurements, the stats and rolls you would use to calculate damage and armor, and he explained how it was essential to work as a team. After that, Demetrius started with a bit of flare, ensuring everyone had what they needed before the game could officially begin.

"All right, we'll start simply." He smiled, setting the scene. "Your troupe of weary travelers has stumbled into a small farming village along the main road. It sits near a stream surrounded by orchards and beautiful golden fields of wheat, and the villagers are kind, noticing you're all looking a bit weary. What they don't know is you've just barely made it to their village, your caravan robbed en route."

"Oh no," one of the craft girls gasped, Chris, smiling at her enthusiasm.

"Oh yes," Demetrius said, raising his hands. "You've come to the village with nothing save the clothes on your back, your worn shoes, and the coin you've somehow managed to hide from the bandits. The villagers are eager to help you, some even bringing food, fresh ale, and sweet honied tea."

"Who are these strangers in *my* village?" Demetrius boomed, his voice lowering. "For I am the Meister and lord of this village. So, who, unlucky travelers, are you?"

"We became lost and followed the wrong road," Chris explained, the others leaning into it.

"We're simple travelers, my lord," one of the teens from the comic shop said, his voice high and strained to emphasize his character. "My name is Morden, bard and fortune teller of some renown. Perhaps I could persuade you to help us with shelter, gracious lord. Just for a couple of nights?"

"Roll for diplomacy," Demetrius instructed, Brandi, Neveah, and the other two new girls watching closely as the teen boy pulled out his D20 and rolled. It luckily landed on a 17, a smile spreading across his face.

"20, not natural," the bard voiced, humming with anticipation.

"I could be persuaded if you'd lend what talents you have to my cause," Demetrius smirked, looking around the table.

Chris became more excited as they played. Brandi, the teen girls from the craft club, and her friend Neveah were all getting into the story. Brandi's elven sorceress complimented Neveah's lawful neutral Paladin quite well, the two girls from the craft club opting for ranger and druid humans. That left the bard, Chris' barbarian, and the final surprising member, a gnomish rogue.

Together they battled a swarm of intruding giant locusts, who threatened the region's entire crop, culminating in a last-minute save from the gnomish rogue's poisoned blade, killing the locust leader and scattering her followers. It was an exciting and seemingly brief three-hour session that left the whole group chatting, laughing, and praising one another until Demetrius called an end, noting that it was already after nine. Soon, parents would be barging through doors demanding their children.

Brandi laughed at this, her face bright and glowing from the fun that night, her friend Neveah equally excited about the next session the following Thursday. It seemed that all the community-requested activities had been a success in their first week, and Chris was beyond grateful to Brandi for encouraging him to go for it.

It was that night, when they were both comfortably nestled in Chris' bed, that he decided to tell her exactly how happy he was. It was somewhat of a risk, and he felt self-conscious but knew Brandi would appreciate it and not judge him if he was awkward. Nevertheless, he'd become so comfortable and happy to be around her that it was too easy to fall into a routine with one another.

"Hey," Chris whispered into the darkness, Brandi moving her head so she was looking up at him. Her head was on his chest again, but now her chin was, her fingers trailing up and down his chest and stomach.

"Hi," she breathed, smiling happily. "What are you thinking?"

"Obvious?"

"You're a thinker, a brooder at times." She smirked, kissing his cheek. "And I find it extremely attractive."

"I wanted to say that… I mean, I just wanted you to know," Chris stumbled, holding her close. "I-I wanted to make sure you knew how much I've enjoyed playing D&D with you."

"Really?" she asked, her eyebrows raised. "Because I really didn't think I was doing that well…."

"Are you kidding? Without that spell to distract the swarm queen, Tyler's gnomish rogue would never have gotten close enough to kill her."

"I mean, I didn't think I was too sure of myself, and I know you've told me to be more confident before," she whispered, kissing his chest softly. "But if you're happy, then I'm happy."

"You're enjoying it, though, right?"

"I am, which is a surprise to both me and Neveah," she giggled, making him smile widely.

"Then I'm very, very happy," he explained, emphasizing it with a kiss. "I hoped we could bond over this, which means a lot."

"Of course," she whispered, kissing his neck now. "I really loved it and can't wait for next week's session."

"Mmm, that's sexy," he sighed, nuzzling her curly hair and inhaling slowly. "Talk nerdy to me…."

"Oh, you're incorrigible," she whispered, snuggling against him again. "It's so late…."

"Get some sleep," Chris encouraged, massaging the small of her back as she relaxed against him. "Tomorrow's Friday, which means date night."

"Incorrigible," she repeated, a sigh escaping her lips as she fell asleep.

Chris loved these moments, the blissful haze between reality and dreams. He loved the feeling of contentment, of letting go and slipping into the warmth of one another's mere existence. This was so much and yet so little, his arms holding her closer as he, too, fell into a hazy sleep. His mind was full of Brandi as he slumbered, unwilling to depart from her arms when they woke to the alarm the following day.

CHAPTER NINETEEN

A couple of weeks had passed since their first D&D session, their third one just ending as Brandi chatted with Neveah before she left the library. She could tell that Chris had really started to enjoy running the library. He seemed to glow, a kindness in his words and actions that wasn't there when she had met him over a month ago. She admired him for his evolution and his passion for community events.

She even noticed that he'd been working more on his own research, encouraging him every step of the way as he told her more and more about the book he wanted to write about archived Victorian African American writers. She was shocked to learn about that part of history and was encouraged and inspired by Chris to learn more. She was also inspired to share more of his interests, and he, in exchange, learned a few of her interests, including romantic dates and cheesy movies.

It was after their D&D match, on the way to his house again, that they started talking about the library and Chris' role there. She hadn't expected him to start talking so openly, happy that he'd let his wall down where she was concerned. Even though he still acted like a know-it-all, he was getting better at accepting help and suggestions from outsiders. She even encouraged him to seek out funding for an assistant. It was good to see Chris become so comfortable and excel at a job he clearly loved.

"I think the community events were the best idea the library has had in a long while," Chris said, walking with her down the sidewalk. "I mean, I'm not taking credit or anything. I'm just saying that the community has started to become more involved with the library, and I like it."

"So do I." She beamed, holding him close as they walked. "I also like that it's made you so happy. You're so hot; you're almost on fire."

"Flatterer." He smirked, kissing her forehead. "And I must admit, I was a bit stupid for hesitating about the suggestions."

"I knew you'd come to that conclusion eventually." She winked, nudging him as they approached his front porch. "Besides, the additions to the community calendar and the upcoming festivals at the church and community center are perfect ways to cross-promote community involvement."

"You're so kissable when you talk about cross-promotion," he laughed, letting her into the duplex with a wink. "But seriously, thanks for pushing me."

"You've always pushed me to be my best, even if I haven't dared to act on it," Brandi admitted, taking her jacket off in the entryway.

"You're so modest; it's almost sickening," he laughed, taking off his bag and jacket before slipping out of his shoes behind Brandi. Once they were comfortable on his couch, they melted into one another's arms.

Brandi could hardly catch her breath, eager to feel his hands and warmth as they kissed. What seemed like moments had turned into an hour, and eventually, the two decided to give in and head to bed early. Brandi was happy to wake and find Chris had already prepared them breakfast and made coffee. They happily chatted over their eggs, toast, and fruit while Chris managed to answer a curious text from Nate, who was in Atlanta for the week on business.

An hour later, after they'd each showered, dressed, and left for their respective jobs, Brandi was contemplating their relationship. It had escalated into something more serious entirely, like a seed sprouting a new tree. Brandi didn't know how to confront it or reconcile with how far she'd fallen in love with Chris.

Until that moment, when she walked through the doors of the daycare, she hadn't realized how much they had started to mean to one another. It felt good, almost impossibly good, and she wondered if, like all good things, it would come to an end. This made her heart sink, and her mind race, the fluttering in her chest amplified when Shea came hurrying up to her in her office during check-ins and drop-offs.

"What's up?" Brandi asked, hoping there wasn't an issue.

"Today's the day," Shea grumbled, rolling her eyes. "Chelsea is here, wanting to volunteer for the day."

"Ugh, of course," Brandi sighed, already exasperated by the thought of Chris's potential job search somewhere other than Sweetgum. It frightened her to the point that she didn't even care about Chelsea being there today. Shea looked a bit concerned, as did the others, but Brandi allowed it, distracted by her current predicament.

It quickly spiraled out of control; Brandi was interrupted for the third time by Chelsea's helpful suggestions. She only ended up confusing the students, annoying the assistants, and wearing Brandi out completely. Chelsea also demanded different lunches and eating a half-hour early to make sure her son stayed on his preferred schedule. The other children were so confused and overwhelmed that many couldn't go down for a nap.

Chelsea's insistence on a shorter nap and her disrespectfully loud YouTube videos during naptime only caused Brandi to lock herself in the office until Chelsea finally left early with Grayson. This was beyond intolerable, and Brandi still had no idea what to do about it.

THAT WEEKEND WAS MORE RELAXING; she and Chris spent Saturday night through Sunday night wrapped up in one another. Chris was beaming about the success of the community events, the library as a whole, and his recent research breakthrough. He was requesting documents from another library for verification, but Brandi was still distracted by her horrible relationship with Chelsea. Something had to give, and even Chris could see she was distracted and hurt.

"Tell me what it is," he whispered, nuzzling her neck gently as he kissed her soft, warm flesh.

"Work stuff," she groaned, unwilling to talk about her horrible Friday. Chris, however, wasn't satisfied with that answer.

"What? The difficult parent, again?"

"Yes, always," she groaned, not looking at him. "She basically took over my daycare Friday, made me look absolutely weak and unprofessional, and drove me to hide in my office until she decided to leave."

"Baby…"

"I know, I know," she admitted, shaking her head. "I have to stand up for myself; I have to confront her; I have to put an end to it all and regain my classroom before she makes me start hating my job."

"Well, you said it…."

"I know, and I really appreciate your encouragement and anger on my behalf," Brandi said, locking eyes with him. "You have no idea how happy I am that you are on my side."

"Always, forever," he said, kissing her lips softly. "You can do this! You're a half-elven sorceress who had to save our entire party the other day with that protection spell."

"You're welcome." She smirked, feeling the weight on her shoulders lessen as they spoke.

It was too short of a weekend, Monday coming around with a double shot of espresso and a hearty hash and potato breakfast at Rochelle's. Chris said goodbye, eager to get set up for the reading hour, while Brandi loathed the idea of having to go to work. It was the first time she'd felt like that in her entire life, and it was infuriating.

Of course, when she got there, Chelsea's car was already in the parking lot, and there was chaos inside the daycare itself. Brandi didn't know what to make of it, hearing some of the kids loudly laughing while others were hiding in corners, unable to handle the stimulation from all the noise. Brandi didn't know what to think, pulling Shea aside to round up the frightened kids while she figured out what the commotion was. It didn't take long to see that Chelsea had brought her son's toy drone in and was doing tricks all over the utterly chaotic classroom.

Brandi couldn't stop herself, striding across the classroom and standing right in front of Chelsea. She didn't seem phased at first, only bringing the drone back when all the other kids had gone silent. She turned it off, setting it down on a nearby table before staring back at Brandi curiously. It was as if she had done nothing wrong and that it was perfectly normal for parents to bring in drones to fly around first thing in the morning.

"It's time for breakfast and morning classes," Brandi said, her voice loud, leaving no room for argument. "The assistants could use help tidying up and settling the kids down."

Chelsea considered her a moment before sighing, turning

from her slowly with a nod. "Yeah, it is getting late; Grayson usually has his breakfast by now."

Brandi was furious, watching as Chelsea only had eyes for her child, unwilling to help Shea or the others get the children seated and their trays ready. In fact, Chelsea handed Grayson a muffin and a carton of milk, and the two of them sat in the corner watching YouTube videos while the rest of the class ate together. Brandi couldn't believe what she was seeing, knowing that if this kept going, she'd have no choice but to explode, the stress of disliking work and avoiding Chelsea finally getting to Brandi.

CHAPTER TWENTY

Brandi could feel the burning in her chest, the anticipation of confrontation mounting as she turned down the street to the new housing development block. They were all nice, one-story homes, with the two-story family homes in the back of the tiny cul-de-sac. The cookie-cutter houses went well with the current town's rustic style, but Brandi had always preferred the old homes built in the mid-century style.

She strode up the wide sidewalk, holding her back tightly to her shoulder as she did. She smiled kindly at a familiar parent from daycare, waving before continuing on to number 1025. That was Chelsea and Grayson's address, and as she got closer, Brandi could feel herself beginning to shake. She absolutely hated confrontation of any sort, but her self-righteous fury and determination would no longer stand aside while Chelsea disrespected her classroom. Chris had been right all along, and though Brandi hated to admit it, she was far too soft.

Perhaps this was her gauntlet, her fiery orientation to a new and more confident Brandi. She didn't know for sure but knew this would be the moment in her favorite books when her quirky protagonist would confront their romantic rival or whatever impediment it was to their love. Of course, Brandi didn't exactly fit this mold, but she was about to confront someone who was an obstacle to her own son's happiness. Perhaps that was a bit harsh, but Brandi would definitely qualify Chelsea as an obstacle in her classroom.

Brandi strode up the sidewalk to the driveway, admiring a cute stone slab walk that led up to their tiny covered front porch and door. She took a deep breath, braced herself, and walked confidently up to the front porch. She didn't mean to, but the knock she had used on the door was a bit too loud. She heard some footsteps inside, no lights on during the middle of the day, but she heard Grayson's voice ring out through the door.

"I'll get it! I'll get it!"

Brandi waited, smiling kindly as Grayson peeped out one of the windows that framed the solid navy-blue door. He was shocked to see her, his eyes wide as he disappeared from the window. The door clicked a couple of times, and then it swung inward, Grayson standing on the welcome mat still in his pajamas. He seemed content in them, the sound of some video game coming from the other room.

"Grayse!" Chelsea yelled from the back of the house, the sound of kitchen utensils clattering. "Who is it?!"

"Miss Brandi!" he called out, smiling at her kindly. "From school!"

"Really?" Chelsea asked, more clanking followed by footsteps as she came around the corner from the large kitchen and dining room in the back of the house. "Oh, it really is you. What are you doing here?"

"We need to talk," Brandi explained, staring directly at her. "We need to talk before the next time you decide to leave your son in *my* classroom."

Brandi made sure to emphasize the word, still not looking

away from Chelsea as she stood there, dumbfounded. Grayson was still curious, watching them from his bedroom doorway, his toys and games loudly beeping beyond. It didn't seem to sink in that Brandi was here officially, Chelsea looking her up and down incredulously. Brandi couldn't help but notice Chelsea's clothes, a simple pair of sweats, a tank top, and the messy wrap around her hair, all accented by a "Kiss the Cook" apron.

"Are you kicking Grayson out of daycare?" she asked outright, still standing in the entrance of their home with the door wide open.

"Of course not. I'm simply telling you that his conversation needs to happen before he can come to class again," she explained, smiling at Grayson calmly. She knew what she wanted to say, and it just came out, like the dam had been broken and the floodwaters were rushing.

"It is the same I would tell any other parent when their child has had a fever and needs to be fever-free for three days before returning to class," Brandi continued, still remaining calm. "Sometimes, a child simply isn't in a state to come to daycare. One of these times is often before the parent is fully in the loop on how I run the classroom. In short, I can't teach Grayson unless you understand my role and your role in *my* classroom."

Chelsea's face was full of indignation and annoyance, but surprisingly, a resignation that Brandi had never seen before. It was shocking, but then Chelsea sighed, stepping aside to let Brandi into their home. It was a lovely little home, the entryway, and hallway extending all the way back to the large archway to the kitchen. The right side of the hall had two doors, one of them being Grayson's bedroom. The other hall wall had a wide-open archway near the door, revealing a plush but stylish living room.

"Come in, please," she said, her smile small and forced. "Would you like something to drink? Coffee? Tea?"

"We have cocoa, too," Grayson piped up, smiling from around the corner of his colorful bedroom.

"Cocoa sounds nice." Brandi smiled; the surprising coldness in that Sunday morning spring air was bracing. During her walk over, she hadn't really noticed it, the adrenaline and anticipation keeping her warm until that very moment.

"Please, let's talk in the kitchen," Chelsea said, her voice tight. She glanced at Grayson, who stayed in his room, understanding that this wasn't a conversation for him.

Once the two were comfortably settled at the small dining table in the large open-concept kitchen, Brandi began, unable to stop herself from trying to find a middle ground. Though she knew she was in the right, Chelsea would have to bend to her classroom rules or withdraw Grayson completely. She realized this wasn't an ideal option for Chelsea, so a comfortable middle ground could be established now that they were both willing to sit down and discuss it.

"So, I think we need to discuss some boundaries and the roles we are expected to fulfill." Brandi smiled, content to sip on the cocoa while Chelsea drank her coffee. "I won't be coy; you must understand that I'm the director and that I'm in charge of the daycare."

"I understand that, but my son isn't just a number in the system," Chelsea replied, defending Grayson. "He has allergies, a strict food schedule, and several other needs that simply must be met."

"He is your son, so I can understand your defensiveness," Brandi said, gently holding the cup on the table. "But tell me, would you appreciate one of the other parents overriding your decisions and changing the classroom in ways that affected not just your child but all the children?"

"I wouldn't like it," Chelsea finally admitted, the silence between them thick like butter.

"Just like you wouldn't like me coming to your job and insisting you change everything about your routine, schedule, and workflow?"

"I guess…" Chelsea sighed, still sounding uneasy. "But we're talking about my child here, not some job that I tolerate to be able to feed and keep my son comfortable. My son is a top priority, and his teachers should also see it this way."

Brandi was becoming annoyed again, Chelsea refusing to realize that she was causing more problems than solving. She didn't want to blow up on her or risk her wrath, but Brandi had become more confident lately, thanks to her friends and Chris. She needed to assert herself, to make sure Chelsea understood her position completely and that it wasn't up for negotiation.

"This is understandable, and you are right; your child's comfort and safety are our top priority," Brandi insisted, her voice firm. "But it is simply unfair and impossible for me to make sure he's having such a specific experience, especially since perfection really isn't achievable. You do understand this, yes? If a custom education and personalized attention and routine is what you are seeking, I can recommend some nannies for you."

"Like I can afford that," Chelsea scoffed, irritating Brandi again. "So, what you're telling me is that my son has to abide by the same rules and routines you, your assistants, and the other children follow? No options for special cases?

"There most certainly are for medical and psychological conditions," Brandi insisted, keeping her voice as firm and steady as possible. This seemed to surprise Chelsea, who was thoughtfully considering her words now. "If there are diet restrictions, medications to keep track of, dispense, and specific coping mechanisms that Grayson needs, we will meet them with as much enthusiasm as possible. That's just our policy. However, you can't expect to come in and take over every little routine we've spent years building."

Chelsea seemed a bit stunned, and the fact that she was mulling over Brandi's words was encouraging. She was a difficult woman and stubborn, but Brandi needed to get through to her. She needed to ensure she understood that it wasn't a situation where the customer was always right. This wasn't a store or restaurant, but a childcare provider's professional assessment and a career Brandi had worked hard at.

"I can understand your position," Chelsea said, her voice low, her tone still hesitant. "I wouldn't want to be told how to do my job."

"Right, so that's why I have the final say," Brandi assured, nodding with encouragement. "I welcome your input, ideas, and your devotion to your child's education. That's often rare, so I applaud you for that. However, you need to understand that I'm the *final* say. You can, of course, request changes and special meals, and Grayson has many options! He's a great kid; just don't dictate changes to me; request them."

"I can respect that," Chelsea admitted, a smile coming to her usually sour face. "And I didn't mean to step on your toes or make you feel like you weren't doing a great job. If I'm being honest, you've done a fantastic job encouraging my son. Grayson has been more talkative, more engaged at home, and he's even talking about daycare and school with excitement."

"I noticed he was quite shy, a reserved child." Brandi smiled, glancing over at the doorway where Grayson was trying to hide and eavesdrop. "But he's a brilliant little boy with a care for others that's quite rare. I hope he learns to cultivate that care."

"He absolutely loves story time and wants me to start reading to him before bed." Chelsea smiled, waving at Grayson, who was grimacing from the doorway. "Right, pumpkin?"

"I like story time, and I'm excited about our trip to the library," he admitted, coming over to stand next to his mom now. "How many books can we get?"

"From the library?" Brandi asked, thinking of the limit that

Everly had imposed on her last year when she had almost a dozen books out at once. "I think the limit is six, but I'll have to ask the librarian."

"Can I get six, and mommy can get six?"

"Technically, yes," Brandi giggled, loving that little Grayson was already enjoying books. They talked about the library, community events at the library, and different things Chelsea and Grayson could get involved with around town. They were still moderately new to the community, and Brandi was happy to help them.

Brandi found herself thinking about how easy all of this was and how she should have done it sooner. Getting Chelsea to understand and cooperate was the gateway to a friendship that Brandi didn't see coming. She and Chelsea sat there for almost a half hour chatting, laughing, and exchanging ideas for outings. She even offered to make the children some special cookies since Grayson was gluten sensitive.

"Oh!" Brandi finally said, hearing a buzz from her phone. "I bet that's the librarian right now asking where I am. I was supposed to meet him today."

"I've seen this librarian," Chelsea smirked, Brandi, blushing. "An interesting addition to the community, wouldn't you agree, Miss Brandi?"

"He's a great librarian." Brandi smiled wryly, moving to stand. "But I'll let you get back to your regular Sunday routine. I've still got lots to do today as well."

"See you tomorrow at school!" Grayson smiled widely, hugging Brandi around the waist when she stood to leave. She laughed, hugging him back and then squatting so she could look directly at him.

"I'll see if I can't persuade the librarian to let you have more than six books," she chuckled, hugging him gently before letting him lead her out to the porch. They spent another few minutes saying their goodbyes before Brandi left, feeling a mixture of relief, happiness, and confidence she hadn't felt in a long time.

"See you both tomorrow morning!" Brandi waved as she left their sidewalk and strode up the block.

CHAPTER TWENTY-ONE

Chris was sitting behind the desk at the library, looking through the newly donated books from the community fund, when his cell phone rang. Although he was surprised he had his ringer on, to begin with, the docile tones of a set of rain beads and the distant clanging of a chime startled one of the patrons reading in the corner. He waved with a grimace, going into the back office to answer.

"Hello, Chris speaking," he said, the number unfamiliar and from out of state.

"Chris, good to speak to you," came a man's voice, deep and authoritative. "I'm Professor Dickson, Curator at Boston University's African American Heritage Museum. How are you today, sir?"

"Ah, Professor Dickson, good to hear from you," Chris said, feeling extremely formal now. He had not expected this call, and his heart was hammering so hard he could feel it in his temple. "I'm well, enjoying the Georgia mountain air in spring, sir."

"Now that sounds lovely," the professor replied, his voice sincere. "I wanted to call you personally to ask if you'd be up for an in-person interview sometime next week?"

"I-I could make the time," Chris affirmed, knowing he still had some frequent flyer miles to cash in. "How about…"

Chris looked over the new calendar in the office, his eyes roaming over community events and commitments before finding that Tuesday was his best day. He wasn't sure if it was too far out, as today was Monday, and Chris really couldn't get away until next week. The thought of ditching Brandi with community day weighed more than he'd care to admit.

"How about Tuesday afternoon, sir? I can catch a flight out of Atlanta first thing and be there after lunch."

"That's reasonable," the professor replied, sounding very enthusiastic. "I look forward to seeing you next Tuesday. And Chris, this is my private line, so please feel free to reach out if you have any questions."

"Absolutely, sir, thank you," Chris said, cupping the back of his neck nervously. "I'll make sure to call if I have any questions."

"Good, I'll see you next Tuesday!" the professor said, his voice a bit too jovial as the line clicked.

Chris couldn't believe it, staring at his phone before saving the number as Professor Dickson. He then had to shake himself out of a temporary haze, opening the office door again and exiting. It was still just the two people who had been in there before, both distracted by their books. He could feel the flush in his face, the nervousness coursing through him until he thought about telling Brandi.

The happiness of actually getting a callback was halted, replaced by a caution he had lost sight of when he heard the professor's name and title. He'd just agreed to an interview in Boston next week for a job he wasn't entirely sure he wanted. Well, that was a lie – he wanted that job because it was quite prestigious, the one he was sure he wouldn't qualify for. After all, he had excellent credentials but no work experience.

He had applied for a few museums in Georgia, in and

around Atlanta, so he could at least stay somewhat close to Sweetgum. This was what he felt he should be doing, getting a chance to explore his relationship with Brandi. However, he worked so hard to get his advanced degree, and history is a competitive field. Chris hadn't received any other callbacks or interview requests from anywhere else and was sure this was the move his career needed.

He also didn't know how to tell Brandi, for whom he had already fallen, and couldn't stop himself from caring for her, even if he wanted to. Chris had enjoyed himself so much on their first date that he'd been texting her after work and chatting with her every time she came into the library. They were becoming inseparable, often taking lunches together and meeting on weekends routinely over the past couple of months. In fact, to say they weren't in a serious relationship would be a lie.

The universe, or God, must have been playing a trick on him in that moment because Brandi came walking into the library with a smile on her face and a gentle wave. Chris didn't know what to think, checking the time to see that it wasn't quite time for her to leave the daycare. It was also far too early for him to close. However, she leaned across the desk, kissed his cheek, and gently laid her hand across his on the desk.

"Hi," she whispered, glancing around at the mostly empty library. "I got out early today. Shea said she'd handle pickup and closing up."

"That's great." Chris smiled, motioning for her to follow him into the office. He couldn't keep it from her and risk hurting her. "I just got off the phone, actually…."

"Oh?" Brandi asked, following him into the office and closing the door partially. She was excited to hear what he had to say, hoping he'd want to do something for the founder's day next month. In fact, she was thinking about how to use his brilliance and education a lot more lately, ever since he talked about his love of history back on their first date.

"I... I got a callback for an in-person interview next week," he said, watching her expression fall. "It's in Boston next Tuesday, and it's the only callback I've had, so... I think I should take the interview. See what they say."

"You'll get it," she assured, her smile wide but wobbly. "You'll have all my love and luck for this interview, and you'll get it. I know you will because you're brilliant, Chris."

"It's very competitive." He smiled, wrapping his arms around her. He could still tell she was sad, her eyes distant, dull as they stood considering one another. "I mean, hey, maybe I won't even get the job."

"Yeah, maybe," she grimaced, kissing his lips gently. "But I have faith in you and your passion."

"Would you like to have dinner tonight?" he asked, nodding out the window. "We can go to Rochelle's, get it to go, and relax in the park. It's a nice night."

"I'd like that," she accepted, wanting to spend as much time with him as possible before next Tuesday.

LATER THAT NIGHT, after they'd departed one another's arms on the park bench, Brandi called her girls. She was happy for Chris and his career, unable to stop smiling even when he was long gone from her sight. However, she was completely devastated and unsure how to cope with these emotions. She was right to take things slow, to take her time, and now she was sitting at her kitchen table crying into her cup of wine while her three best friends sat by helplessly.

"It's not fair," Neveah finally said, shaking her head. "He basically led you on, and now he's just leaving."

"I wouldn't put it quite like that," Joanne said, sipping on her glass of white wine.

"But essentially, that's how Brandi feels," Courtney said, reaching over to offer her another tissue as she sobbed silently.

"He's thinking of his passions, his career, and his calling," Joanne tried to explain, both Neveah and Courtney unwilling to offer him a kind word. "You can't blame him for wanting what he wants."

"But we can blame him for being careless with our best friend's heart!" Neveah spat, shaking her head.

"It's n-not like t-that e-exactly," Brandi whimpered, drying her eyes and blowing her nose. Joanne offered her another tissue as the four sat around the small living room coffee table. "I knew to take it slow; I knew not to get so invested, and I ignored it. I let myself fall for him, to think that we had a future, but once again, my imagination has gotten the better of me."

"He's not a saint," Courtney said, trying to find a middle ground as she sipped her red. "But he's probably just as torn about this as you are. Did you stop to consider that?"

"He doesn't seem like it," Brandi said, becoming bitter now. "He acted like I simply should know, all matter-of-fact."

"Well, we've all kind of noticed that he's like that," Joanne said, offering another fresh tissue. "Curt, thoughtful, calculated, and perhaps a bit too prideful."

"Your type," Neveah sighed, downing the rest of her drink and munching on some trail mix from the bowl. "He's not in my good book right now."

"He's got to focus on what he wants, even if that isn't a life in small-town Sweetgum with the girl he is clearly in love with," Courtney sighed, making them all look at her. "It's true! Anyone can see they're mad about one another, true love and all that…."

"Then you have to talk to him," Neveah insisted, pointing to her phone. "Text him, tell him you should get together some-time soon, and just outright ask him about it."

"A bit blunt, but that's the only way to know what he's thinking or what he says he's thinking," Courtney said, patting Brandi's arm. "Just be honest with Chris and yourself."

"I don't even know what to say," Brandi sighed, being reminded of those crisis moments in her favorite novels. "Run to him? Play a heartfelt song or perhaps just vomit words of love and devotion?"

"Whatever you want to do, just make sure he understands your feelings just as well as you do," Joanne smiled, leaning over to hug her gently. "You're not helpless, you know? You've got us."

"I know, I know," she sighed, wrapping her arms around them as they came in for a group hug. "I love you girls so much...."

"Awe, we love you too," Joanne assured, smiling happily. "Now come on, chin up. Send him a text and drink the rest of your wine like a big girl."

"Hilarious," Brandi snickered, realizing they were treating her just like she treated one of her students. It was ironic but the exact thing she needed in that moment.

It wasn't until later, when they'd all gone after midnight, that she really broke down. She was in a warm bath, and all she could think of was Chris leaving. Chris finding a co-worker in Boston who understood him better, who he could love. A life, and a future, far away from the simple one Brandi was living here in Sweetgum. She was being silly, she knew it, but she loved him and couldn't imagine not seeing him every day.

She'd tried so hard not to get attached, to take everything glacially slow, but failed. Her heart dived in, dragging her along for the ride, and her tears freely fell into that now lukewarm bubble bath. She could barely wipe away her tears as she got out, got ready for a restless night, and lay in bed, sobbing, for the next couple of hours. She didn't know when she fell asleep, but it frightened her when she saw she'd missed her alarm and two phone calls the next morning.

One was from Shea, who opened and started intake without her an hour ago. The second was from Chris, who saw her message from last night about meeting up. She was nervous, standing in her disheveled sweats and tank top as she read his text.

BRANDI:

Chris, can we meet up this weekend before you leave for Boston?

CHRIS:

Of course, let's meet up Sunday and spend all day together, okay? Sorry I didn't respond until this morning! I was so tired last night.

Brandi bit her lip at this, happy they'd spend all day together but unsure what she'd say. She didn't want to really stop him from pursuing his passions and dreams, and she'd never forgive herself if he grew to hate her for it. On the other hand, she'd also hate to see their love sour, as sweet as it was now. Maybe, like her friends suggested, she needed to understand her own emotions first.

BRANDI:

Sounds good! It can be like a little going away party between you and me.

She didn't know how else to respond or how to wish him love and luck on his journeys. She truly wished him nothing but love and happiness, and if that meant that he had to find it outside of Sweetgum, then she really had no right to ask him to stay. She knew this and was trying to figure out the best way to convey her love and acceptance of his choice, even if her heart was breaking into tiny pieces.

CHAPTER TWENTY-TWO

Chris was distracted the whole car ride from Sweetgum to Atlanta International Airport. Sunday was still fresh in his mind; the entire situation seemed to spiral and finally settle at a point that Chris wasn't entirely sure he was comfortable with. The events of Sunday seemed to be replaying themselves on a loop as he navigated lanes of traffic and winding county roads toward the state's cultural capital.

He remembered texting Brandi early, meeting her at Joanne's coffee shop just after eight. They both seemed a bit nervous, which Chris expected, but what he didn't expect was Brandi to wish him luck with his new job. She was so resolute, so somber, that it truly did feel like a going away party between the two of them. They were just wrapped up in each other, talking quietly, saying sweet soft things about their shared memories over the past few months. It was good, something Chris loved every moment of as he'd yet to make up his mind about this job.

However, the day spiraled out of control when his sister-in-law, her eldest child, and his mother entered the coffee shop before church. Chris was mortified by the three nosey women asking all sorts of questions about their plans for the day, what she thought of Chris' interview, and all sorts of things while they waited for their coffee order.

Brandi looked flattered, a bit embarrassed, and entirely overwhelmed, but she handled it gracefully; Chris stepped in to tell them they had plans together and should be leaving. But, of course, he didn't expect his grandmother, father, brother, and nephew to be outside waiting. This prompted a quick succession of protests followed by the kidnapping of both Chris and Brandi to church and then the after-church dinner at his granny's.

Brandi was ecstatic to spend time with Everly and to meet his family as far as he could tell, but he bitterly hated their interference in what was probably their last day together in Sweetgum. That thought alone drove Chris to abruptly excuse them both during dessert. Brandi had been confused and slightly startled, but once they were out of earshot, walking around the block, just the two of them, Chris apologized.

What struck him was she wasn't annoyed or unhappy about their little detour, welcoming his family's intrusion with grace and enthusiasm. He didn't understand why and as he drove, weaving through the highway interchanges, his mind dwelt on a single thing she'd said that day right before leaving him on their walk around the corner from his granny's.

She wasn't saying everything, that he was sure, but the surety with which she said goodbye to him was devastating. Like a hole had started a leak in his chest, and he couldn't quite catch his breath.

"I appreciate meeting your family and everything, and I'm already sad about your departure." She had smiled, stopping on the sidewalk to stare up at him. "But I respect your decision to chase your passions, and I am happy to have been a brief part of it."

She walked away after that, leaving him with a lingering kiss and a small smile. He watched her go, clutching her small bag over her shoulder as the midday sun glittered off her brown eyes. He watched her until she disappeared from view, his heart plummeting when he realized what she meant by all that.

Even now, as he parked the car in the long-term parking, took the shuttle to the security line, and slipped off his shoes, he was thinking about her reaction. He was thinking about the implications of her words and the true feelings she held behind her brilliant brown orbs. He thought about her trilling laugh when he whispered into her ear. He remembered the blush on her cheeks when he said something suggestive and loved how her face lit up when he entered a room.

His interview later that day went well; Professor Dickson had nothing but kind and curious words for his research and book. The Professor was a curious man who seemed genuinely interested in diversifying and bringing to light the African American historical characters that most people weren't taught or introduced to in a traditional educational setting. Chris had always thought that was a shame, and luckily, Professor Dickson agreed.

They enjoyed themselves, discussing various subjects of interest for over an hour before the professor had a course to teach. Chris thanked him for his time, but as soon as he left the elaborate and beautifully adorned faculty offices, all he could think of again was Brandi.

The next few days in Boston were full of contemplation, thinking about what it would be like to live here. He couldn't feel excited about the prospective job the entire time he was in Boston. It was all a blur, peppered with the yearning to call Brandi and clear the air. This trip wasn't about her, though, something he kept telling himself as he roamed the city's many museums, libraries, and significant collections.

He knew that he should feel excited about the opportunity. This is a great career move for him, especially since he is so early in his career. But all he could think about was how much he would be losing. He didn't want to give up his life in Sweetgum, and to his final surprise, he didn't want to give up Brandi. The thought of holding her in his arms, kissing her lips, and hearing his voice on her tongue was beyond description or reason.

Until that moment, when he was sitting in that Boston café sipping some mediocre coffee, he didn't realize that some things in life are more important than a prestigious career. If he were really meant to take this job, then he'd be excited. He might be conflicted, but he would also be excited or happy. Unfortunately, he wasn't, and that should have been an immediate red flag.

He was crushed thinking about the possibility of relocating, forfeiting any future he had with Brandi in his hometown. Even if he changed his mind later, forgoing the career and returning, it wouldn't be fair to ask her to wait for him. It also wouldn't be fair to his family, this bouncing like an uncertain backpacker through Europe.

It was when he returned to his hotel, ready to call Brandi, that the hiring manager from the museum called Chris. Professor Dickson was friendly, intrigued during their interview, and was even more friendly when he called Chris that afternoon.

"Chris! How are you? How do you find Boston?"

"It's a beautiful and old city, sir." Chris smiled, impressed by New England's architecture and vast historical collections.

"I've got good news for you!" Professor Dickson said, Chris going still. "We'd like to invite you back for a second interview with the understanding that this is just a formality. The team was very impressed with your dissertation, research, and willingness to relocate and are eager to move forward and offer you the position."

"Sir, I appreciate the offer, but I'm going to have to take

myself out of the running," he said, his voice firm, a smile spreading over his lips. "I just can't make the move at this time in my life."

"Ah, I see...." Professor Dickson drawled, his voice soft. "Thank you for telling me, Chris. I have to admit; I am a bit disappointed. However, I will say this – if you ever want to make the move to Boston, reach out to me personally. Maybe we can talk more in the future and work something out until another position opens up."

"I will remember that professor," Chris assured, grabbing his small laptop bag and suitcase from the hotel closet. He wasn't supposed to leave for three more days, but he had to get back. "And thank you again for the opportunity. I will be in touch again. Your research about African American spies during the Revolutionary War has sparked my interest."

"I'll remember that," Professor Dickson joked, a jovial laugh on his lips. "Keep in touch, and good luck, Chris."

CHAPTER TWENTY-THREE

Brandi's day had been a long one. The children were uncommonly unruly today as the aids and even Chelsea, who was volunteering a lot, became overwhelmed. It must have been a full moon or perhaps a phase because all of them were exhausted when Chelsea and Grayson were the last to leave. Brandi heaved a sigh of relief before taking a long slow walk back home. She didn't feel like going to the library to see Mrs. Everly, who was back at the library begrudgingly. She had been cranky since Chris left for Boston a few days ago. Like Brandi, Mrs. Everly wished him nothing but love and luck, but secretly, she wanted him to stay.

It couldn't be helped; the ache in her heart from his absence weighed like a stone. But it was only a few days, and he said he'd be back whether he got the job or not, so at least she'd see him again. She hoped she could at least spend one day and night with him before he left, a real farewell and well-wishing before he disappeared from her life. Thinking of him that way, always keeping herself in check, was all she could do now not to start crying over his loss.

It was a bit pathetic, and Brandi loathed this part of herself.

She'd become so attached, so blinded by her heart's desire, that she hadn't considered the consequences of failure. She had been ignorant, a bit naïve, and entirely too eager to break her own heart, which was a hard lesson to learn. Of course, this being her first real love, it would linger the longest. Perhaps thirty years from now, when she hopefully had her own grandchildren, she could warn them about the fragility of their hearts. A whimsical idea like that made her smile as she rounded the block toward her home. She was close, the warm spring afternoon welcoming her with ambrosia, pine, and wildflowers.

She was not expecting to spot someone standing on her front porch, pausing when she recognized a familiar pair of broad shoulders. It was Chris, standing there with a bouquet of flowers and a wide smile. He wasn't supposed to be home for three more days, but she didn't care. She didn't hide her happiness, jogging up the sidewalk to the porch to smile up at him brightly.

"Hey, you..."

"What are you doing here?" she asked, wanting to reach out and hold him so badly. Instead, she kept her trembling hands on her bag strap.

"I don't want to leave Sweetgum," he admitted, her breath hitching in her throat. "I mean, not just Sweetgum, of course. My family, my friends, the library, and... I want to build a life here, y-you see?"

Brandi wasn't entirely sure what he was trying to say, but her heartbeat was thundering in her ears. She had hoped those words would escape his lips, those three little words that changed entire worlds. Those three little words that would forever change who she was and what Chris meant to her lingered, unspoken, as he fumbled further with a cute blush and stammer.

"I'm trying to say that I want to build a life here, and after being away for so long in California, I feel like this is where my home really is," he explained, his bright eyes wide. "I want to stay close, in Sweetgum, w-with you. I... I love you, Brandi."

Tears immediately flooded her eyes, desperately trying to blink them back as he confessed. She wrapped her arms around his neck with a tremble, her lips finding his happily as they held one another close. It wasn't until she pulled away, lips swollen and shuddering from the sheer force of his love, that she was able to reciprocate his feelings.

"I love you, too," she whispered breathlessly, the glow about him magnifying so brightly that it was hard not to smile back at him. They shared another passionate, loving kiss on the stoop now, the flowers still in his hand as he wrapped his arms around her.

"Eh-hem," came a noise from behind them. The two pulled away with a blush, looking toward the road.

To their amusement, standing on the sidewalk was a half-dozen older women, Mrs. Everly smirking as the young couple held one another closely, waving coyly at Chris and Brandi.

"Not going to duck into a bush and pretend you don't see me, Granny?" Chris asked, his voice full of laughter.

"Well, now that you two seem to be done playing hard-to-get with each other," Mrs. Everly called, the other older women smirking and giggling. "I don't think I have to play sick anymore!"

"I knew it!" Chris laughed, Brandi positively ecstatic to see both Mrs. Everly and Chris so amused. She giggled with them, holding Chris close as his hand snaked around her waist.

"Grandma, have you really been trying to set us up this whole time?" Chris asked, walking with Brandi toward the group of chattering and giggling older women.

Mrs. Everly smiled, her friends nudging her to tell the truth. She sighed, waving them away to chat privately with Chris and Brandi. The older ladies were hesitant but slowly walked on, waiting for Everly at the end of the block.

"Fine, you've figured me out," she finally said, touching Chris' face gently. "I thought you two would be good together, and I didn't want my baby Chrissy here to leave again."

"You faked weeks of sickness to hook me up with your eligible grandson?" Brandi asked, Mrs. Everly looking a bit sheepish now.

"You disapprove my romantic little owl?" she asked, pushing some hair back from Brandi's face.

"Never," she said, wrapping her arms around Mrs. Everly. "I've always wanted to call you granny."

"Marriage already?" Mrs. Everly whispered in her ear, hugging her back excitedly. "I like the way you think."

To her surprise and utter happiness, Chris pulls Brandi into his arms, smiling down at her with curious eyes. "What are you two conspiring about now?"

"Love, my love," Brandi interjected, making Mrs. Everly smirk. "And family."

"So, I take it you didn't get the job in Boston?" Mrs. Everly asked, looking a bit dismayed now. She was an expert at changing the subject, even if it was sometimes blunt.

"Well, I did, actually," Chris smirked, both his granny and Brandi staring at him.

"So, you are leaving?" Mrs. Everly questioned, looking between the couple.

"You don't have to worry about that, Grandma," Chris admitted, lovingly brushing the back of his slender fingers over Brandi's cheek. "As long as Brandi wants me, I'll never need to be anywhere but Sweetgum."

EPILOGUE

Chris stood behind the desk at the library, checking in books as the quietness of the end of a long day seemed to entrance him. He was glad that he still had all this time at the library, his grandmother enjoying her time off so much that she actually retired. It was a long-time coming; the woman was eager to enjoy the freedom of retirement. Chris was more than happy to take over the library for her, though, applying for the job, with her recommendation, the moment it went up for bid online.

Of course, he had some competition from a few interested parties from the Atlanta suburbs, but his research, recommendations from Professor Dickson and his grandmother, as well as the over-qualified nature of his application, meant he was the obvious choice. He truly enjoyed it, and because of his expansion over the past few months for the community, the county has agreed he could take on an assistant. Chris liked this idea a lot, a promising young college grad from Sweetgum eager to help out close to home.

He had also followed his own passions and research, having more time to dedicate when his assistant took the not-so-busy mornings on weekdays to allow him his studies. This time has helped so much with the books he'd been writing. In addition, with support from Brandi and Professor Dickson, he's undertaken an extensive research project on unpublished manuscripts from Black authors of the Victorian era and how many of these had been archived by library systems across the country.

He was still trying to figure out the full scope of the book he was writing, but he was enjoying the research and loved the balance in his life. He spent the morning working on research for his book, the afternoon running the library and its various community events, and then in the evenings, he saw Brandi's smiling face. He loved this most of all, thinking how lucky he was to have such a life. He truly felt at peace and in love, and Brandi seemed so happy to support him and his research.

Of course, Chris was adamant about expanding on to her daycare and perhaps one day creating a second one in the neighboring town. He wanted her to have everything she wanted, and he really admired her passion for teaching children. It was something he'd always had an interest in but from a historical standpoint. She, however, wanted to ignite their curiosity and that was something she excelled at.

Just then, his phone dinged, looking down to see a text from Brandi.

MY LOVE:

Do you want me to bring anything over tonight?

CHRIS:

Just my beautiful, smart, sexy, romantic, flawless angel of a girlfriend...

A little fantastical today?

Always when it comes to you.

Chris chuckled at their texts, relieved when the day finally ended, and he could spend the evening with Brandi. He was preparing the kitchen when there was a knock at his door. Brandi had shown up for dinner like they'd been doing several times a week for a few months now. They enjoyed their meal of barbeque chicken, homemade mac and cheese, and Rochelle's famous potato salad before cuddling up together on his couch in front of one of their favorite new streaming series.

"How's the book going?" she asked, snuggling against him.

"I've discovered another lead today by looking through the archives sent from a large library in Tennessee," he admitted, excited about the new thread that needed to be pulled. "How about you? How are things going at the daycare and with Chelsea?"

Brandi grinned at this and explained how Chelsea struggled initially, but now she was easy to get along with. She was even following Brandi's directions when she came in to help out as a room mom. Brandi and Chris both laughed at this, exchanging soft kisses and sighs before Brandi continued.

"Now that she isn't trying to undermine me, her ideas are actually really great. For example, she had an idea today for a craft project the children could do to go with a book we're reading," Brandi sighed, kissing his neck. "I thought it was a great idea for someone without classroom experience. It's a great cross-curriculum idea that will really get the children to engage with books in a new way."

After a few more minutes, Chris decided to execute his plan that evening. He'd been planning it with his assistant, grandmother, and Nate all day. He convinced Brandi to walk over to the library with him, the two of them enjoying the warm summer night. She followed him down the street to the library, chatting about Chelsea, the book club, and her excitement to branch out into community events.

When they finally made it to the library and went inside, Brandi gasped in astonishment. Chris had decorated the library with tons of twinkling fairy lights, and there was a table covered with a bright white tablecloth. A massive bouquet of Brandi's favorite flowers sat in the center of the table, and leading up to the table; there were flower petals scattered. They formed a sort of runner for her to follow as the couple stepped closer.

"Chris, what is this?" Brandi asked, her eyes still wide and full of happy tears.

Chris smiled, took her hand, and led her to the table. He then took a ring box off the table and got down on one knee. The elation in her eyes was something he'd remember for the rest of his life, the way her lip trembled when he smiled up at her and took her hand delicately.

"Brandi Astore," he said, opening the box to reveal a simple black onyx band with a bright glittering pear-shaped diamond. "Will you do me the greatest honor and become my bride?"

"Chris!" She smiled, wrapping her arms around him, the two falling to the floor with laughter. "Of course! Of course, I will. Yes, yes, yes...."

Their lips meet feverishly as they hold one another on the thinly padded floor, making Chris chuckle when he finally pulled away from her. She seemed absolutely speechless now, allowing him to prop himself on his arm and slip the beautiful ring on her finger.

"Yes?" he asked, kissing her fingers delicately.

"Always yes."

AUTHOR'S NOTE

Thank you so much for reading Sweet Sunsets, the second book in the Sweetgum Meadows Romance series of stand-alone novels. I really hope you loved it! If you enjoyed this book, please consider leaving it a review so that others may also find it. Also, if you haven't read Kim and Malik's story yet, check it out today!

I look forward to introducing you to the other characters in this lovely, family-oriented town where each couple will find their happily ever after. So join me with book 3, Infinite Kiss, to watch Courtney find her happily ever after.

Would you like to receive bonus scenes and keep up with what's next with my upcoming books? Then, make sure you sign up for my mailing list on my website by visiting ImaniPrice.com.

ALSO BY IMANI PRICE

Book 1: Love Between Us

Book 2: Sweet Sunsets

Book 3: Infinite Kiss

Book 4: Dance With Me

Book 5: In Charge

Book 6: Forever With You

Book 7: Secret Sweethearts

Book 8: Endless Love

Book 9: The Harder We Fall

Book 10: Reservations of the Heart

Book 11: Play by Play

Book 12: Guarded Hearts

Book 13: Healing Hearts

Book 14: Dear Sweetgum

Book 15: Lanterns of the Meadows (novella)

Book 16: Drawn to You

Book 17: Under the Sweetgum Tree

Sweetgum Meadows' Visitor's Guide

My full audiobook catalog is available for FREE on YouTube. Check it out here: https://swiy.co/Sweetgum

To all my lovely readers,

Thank you for reading